BLOOD LEGENDS

REBIRTH

KIM PETERSEN

Blood Legends: Rebirth. © copyright 2020 Whispering Ink Press

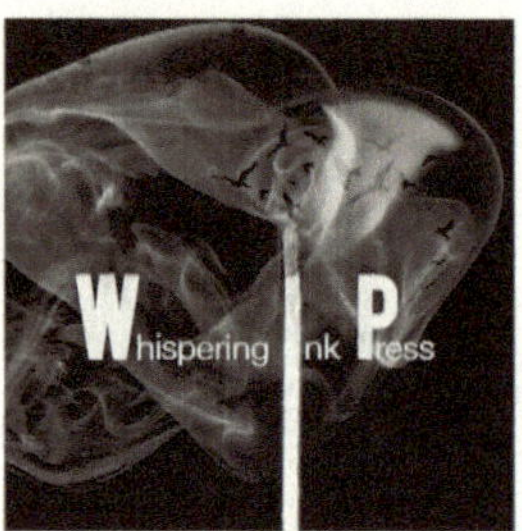

eBook IBSN: 978-0-6485491-8-5

Paperback IBSN: 978-0-6485491-9-2

Edited by Paul Vander Loos

Cover Art by Paradox Book Designs

For my clan Julian, Jordan, Ashlan, Indiana and Lakota.
I love you.

BLOOD LEGENDS
REBIRTH

USA Today Bestselling Author
KIM PETERSEN

Introduction

Promises made by the undead remained undead. A mysterious prophecy has come to pass with the arrival of a newborn baby.

The survival of the vampire clan is now threatened with the rebirth of a long-buried species. The Lygarou have reawakened with an unquenchable thirst for blood. The next full moon is looming and Jett has no choice but to face the reckoning.

He must find and kill the wolf-mother and her baby before his sire destroys the only person remaining in his life worth living for. But when Jett unearths the truth about the Lygarou bloodlines, he is forced to face a choice that will forever altar the future and question his loyalty toward the clan.

Can Jett risk all that matters to him on a future paved with uncertainty? Or will his loyalty to the clan prevail?

Rebirth is an urban fantasy set in a post-apocalyptic world from bestselling author Kim Petersen, the second book in the *Blood Legends*: Ground Zero series.

CONTENTS

DARK CHAMBERS

Indifference felt like cold armor. Hunger gripped me. *Exhausting.* My mind contorted. I squeezed my eyes shut and hung my head. Strangled sobs tormented me. Each cry stoked the insatiable need to feed on their blood. My veins palpitated beneath my skin. I shivered and groaned as I shifted my back against the sandstone wall. My ass was paralyzed.

Avila's body curled on the ground. Her head was heavy in my lap and she trembled in a fitful slumber. Candlelight offended my senses. Sun's voice rasped over my pulse.

"Is this how it ends for us – starving in a filthy airless cell mocked by our food?" She gave a rueful laugh.

I lifted my chin to look at her beside me. Her skin

was like chalky mesh sunk against cheekbones. Her hair fell in dull yellow clumps, almost concealing the stony eyes peering back at me. She licked chafed lips and flicked her chin toward the opposite cell. It was crammed with humans. There must have been about fifty of them.

"I can't tell which side was better."

I squinted toward the other cell. My joints ached; especially my knuckles as I clenched and unclenched them. The scent of fear and sweat carried along the shadowy shaft separating the cells. It hurt to look at them. Their offerings were too much to bear.

"Neither."

My gaze lingered on a woman who stood pressing her forehead against the rusty steel bars. Grimy fingers clutched the metal posts; burnt-red hair like straw. Brown eyes ebbed as she blinked at me. My ears pricked with the sound of her thumping heart. My mouth watered. I tore my eyes away from her and swallowed hard.

"We're all living the nightmare no matter which side we're on."

Sun grazed a hand across my arm. Her skin was like ice.

"I'm on your side, that's all that counts."

Emptiness gripped me when I looked at her. Time

had lost meaning. *How long had we been here? Weeks? Months?* Endless time snatched in the shadows and feeding on sewer rats. We were prisoners now; thrown in the putrid cells beneath the city with the humans they hunted and collected. It was punishment for betraying Marius. I deserved it, but Avila and Sun didn't.

My eyes locked onto hers.

"I'm ... sorry."

I'm so sorry.

She shook her head.

"Don't be." She leaned in closer as the sound of stomping boots drifted along the tunnels. "Remember what you told me; don't let them take your soul, Jett."

"What soul?"

She said nothing but her darkening stare conveyed her thoughts. The truth was my soul was sucked into a black abyss the day Scarla was murdered. It was the same day I'd made the choice to die. But even the apathy accompanying my human death couldn't erase the agony she left behind. Everything was meaningless without her.

Death could claim me again.

I looked away from Sun as Avila stirred. She sat up, stretching over sickly pale features and pitted eyes. Dark hair brushed at her waist as she cocked her head.

"The guards are coming." Her voice was hoarse.

"Yes."

Her eyes widened at me. Fangs glinted as she winced before she made the move to stand up. Her legs buckled slightly when she extended an arm toward me.

"Get up."

My girl.

She was the only reason I had to keep going. I reached for her hand and hauled myself up, steadying myself against the wall. I felt like cardboard. Weakness crept through me, but I ignored it as a low rumble began to rise among the human captives across the way.

High pitched shrills and disembodied wails erupted as they began clawing at one another in an effort to distance themselves from the cell entrance. Terror was an intoxicating emotion. Excitement rimmed.

"The vampire guards are coming!"

"God, help us ... Please, no!"

Limbs entangled. A few of them fell beneath the panicking mob. The blunt sound of crushing bones was a distinct melody in my ear. My gaze found the woman who still clutched the cell bars. Ragged lips mumbled breathless secrets. Her eyes were closed. She appeared in another world.

Sun stood beside me. We exchanged a look before I pushed off the wall and walked toward the cell bars. I stopped across from the woman and watched her, tuning out to the chaotic fever and the laughter that echoed along the tunnel walls as the guards drew closer.

She shifted her weight from side to side and squeezed her eyes shut even tighter. Her shoes were made of worn brown leather and fringed a pair of torn denim jeans. She flung her head back. Grime appeared like patchwork over the skin of her throat. Her words became frantic. Louder.

"Lygarou ... Lygarou ... the prophecy is born ... the city will burn to ashes."

Avila and Sun sidled up either side of me. Screams escalated. Mayhem like wild alley cats. My heart pounded. My fangs ached for blood. Four guards rounded the bending shaft and came into view. Avila stiffened.

"Lygarou?"

I shrugged. My gut curdled as I looked back at her. She froze suddenly. Shadows flickered across her face like an apparition as she steadied her gaze on me. Lips spoke cryptic messages.

"I've seen the birth of a Lystalker – the half-breed. She's arrived to ignite the Legends of Blood."

"Legends of Blood?"

I frowned and gripped the steel bars. The guards halted between the cells. They were clad in the usual black leather attire customary to the kindred. Chunky boots adorned their feet and twisted on the damp ground. They had their backs to me.

The woman's eyes darted toward the guards. They sniggered and cackled, nudging one another as they surveyed the humans. The prisoners quietened, albeit for a man who lay curled and groaning on the floor. Blood oozed from his skull and spilled over his fingers as he clutched the wound.

Thirst stabbed my stomach like a serrated knife.

I looked back at the woman as one of the guards hissed and held up a set of keys, shaking them. He laughed even louder when some of the people sobbed, shrinking further into the shadows. Just as the cell gate creaked open, the woman took a quick breath before she mouthed two words at me: "Blood Legends."

Blood Legends.

A chill went through me. Mysterious predictions and farfetched superstitions haunted me. They were the same words that had passed from the ginger-beard hawker before I tore his head from his neck. Words that foretold a time of reckoning that would bring the kindreds undone. Our greatest existential threat.

I had to know more.

Two of the guards converged on the human prisoners. The crowd instantly became restless. A few women screeched as the guards hunched over them, hissing before ensnaring sharp talons around their arms and dragging them closer.

I looked away. My attention was captured by the guards that had turned our way and were now opening our cell door. All thoughts of Blood Legends and folklore evaporated as eyes the color of bright lemons pierced into me.

Conceit. I could smell it. He leaned against the cell bars and regarded us with a dark grin. His mouth was a shock of scarlet, parting to reveal stained fangs. His crony had a neck like a bull. He grunted and pushed into the cell behind lemon-eyes, stopping with a sneer. An inky stare settled on Sun.

"It appears as if fortune has bestowed upon you this day." Lemon-eyes ran bony fingers through his hair, giving his head a toss for good measure.

"How so?" Avila gripped her hips and glared.

His grin widened. Screams shattered my ears. I looked back at the other cell to see the guards hauling three prisoners from the chamber. Two women; one man. The redheaded woman was among them. Lemon-eyes' voice grated into my bones.

"The Masters have decided it is time for your citation. You are to have an audience with Master Zaros."

Zaros? The name was unfamiliar. My thoughts

scattered as the three humans were shoved into our cell. They stumbled and immediately cowered together as the guards returned to the other cell. Hunger overwhelmed me as I eyed the fresh blood now within arm's reach.

"Yes ... you are permitted to feed before your attendance." Lemon-eyes motioned toward the man and two women who began to sob uncontrollably. Not the redhead though. She stood trembling but her eyes daggered into mine when I looked at her.

Lygarou. They're coming; the prophecy holds true. I can show you.

The words weren't spoken yet I heard them clearly. I turned to see the guards dragging the wounded humans from the other chamber. Some of them were dead. Agonizing wails reverberated all around.

Lemon-eyes spoke again.

"Well; what are you waiting for?" he laughed. "You must be famished. Your feast awaits you."

Sun and Avila didn't hesitate. Desperation was like a vapor as they moved forward. The guards yanked the injured who were still alive over the cell threshold, dumping them near my feet. My eyes darted back to the woman. Her gaze widened. My pulse screamed as I stepped forward.

"Wait!"

All eyes turned on me. I squared my chin and gestured toward the woman.

"That one is of use to the Masters. Let her live."

"Why?" Lemon-eyes glared. Talons twirled the ends of his hair.

"Because she's a witch with valuable knowledge."

The guards laughed but Lemon-eyes didn't. He slinked closer to me. Eyes like deadly firestones burned into mine.

"What knowledge does the witch possess?"

"She knows about the Blood Legend prophecy."

His features twisted and paled beneath the dim light.

"Very well. We shall inform the Masters." He flicked a wrist toward his cronies. "Return her and fetch another!"

An odd sense of relief flooded through me. My gaze fell to the groaning man at my feet. I bent to my knees and gripped his head roughly. My pulse quickened. Anticipation had never been so sweet. My fangs sunk into human flesh and reprieve was mine. I fed like a demon.

Hunger did have a soul. It was created from human flesh and blood, and death was its heart.

And it owned me.

2

TREASON HAS A SCENT

"**W**ell, well, look at what the fangbangers dragged in!"

The guards halted abruptly either side of us. Lemon-eyes tittered. They'd led us down a series of dank tunnels that eventually gave way to an open burrow deep beneath the city. It was part of the subway grid.

My boots scuffed against gravel. Sun and Avila stopped either side of me as I searched for the speaker who I assumed to be Zaros. I saw no one. *Moths.* Their wings sounded like an acoustic tune as they sought out flames.

Fact: *They don't hand out instruction manuals when you turn kindred. Humanity eludes me. I'm not sure how I feel about that yet.*

The area was spacious. My senses flared with stale

air and candlewax; burning candles balanced on wrought iron candelabras. Shadows stretched and writhed over black glyphs and symbols across the walls. Red satin adorned lengthy lounges and appeared viable. The kindred loved red. Perhaps it was because the color now represented our lifeforce.

My gaze lingered on scarlet satin. I felt heady. *Drunk.* Fresh human blood fused in my veins. It was euphoric. I shook my head. I had to keep it together. *Who knew what they had in store for us?* Provocative sensations and red visions shattered when the throaty voice spoke again.

"I detect the scent of treason in the air."

I frowned and whirled toward the sound of the speaker, spotting a dark figure doused in the shadows in a far corner.

"What say you, Blade?" The figure stepped forth and lingered at the edge of the gloom. Onyx eyes glimmered. Thick pearly fangs were the next thing I saw as he grinned. "How would you describe the stench of treason?"

Fact: *Lemon-eyes has a name.*

Blade's lanky figure shifted. A satanic smile erupted as he tossed his long mane and looked at us. His nostrils were like a bonfire.

"Worse than the decaying rats they've been feeding on."

The bullnecked vampire chuckled as he gripped Sun's arm and pulled her closer.

"This one smells like a canary." A chunky tongue swept across meaty lips. "I always had a thing for little birdies."

She scowled and yanked her arm free.

"Take your *thing* elsewhere, dipshit. I'm no birdie."

He responded with a hiss. I grimaced. His breath was distinguishable even from my position on the other side of Sun. It was disgusting.

Laughter chilled me to the core.

"Now, now, children, there will be plenty of time to play later."

I got my first real glimpse at him as he emerged entirely from the shadows. A short clump of jet hair spread over his scalp and shone almost violet above ebony skin. An engraved silver buckle was all that broke the black leather covering all his body. Bejeweled fingers stroked his jaw as he regarded us.

He was striking ... captivating. But I didn't dwell on his appearance too long. My thoughts were stolen by more urgent affairs. Like how was I going to get us out of this mess for one?

The dark vampire tilted his head.

"But first we must tend to the matter at hand." He grinned. "We must decide the fate of our betrayers."

Question: *How could I be deemed a betrayer when I felt nothing for the kindred?*

Answer: *It didn't matter. I was a pawn beneath vampire law now, whatever that meant.*

Suddenly he was in front of me and breathing in my face. Black eyes flashed red. "I am Zaros." His stare crept over Avila and Sun before settling back on me. I tried not to swallow visibly. "No doubt you have heard of me?"

I shook my head.

"Can't say that I have."

"Regardless, I am to decide your misfortune for your actions against the clan."

"Have we not experienced enough misfortune rotting and starving in that deplorable cell for weeks on end?"

He leaned closer. "And you think that is adequate penance for intentionally discarding the one vial of AB positive blood known to exist?"

I held his gaze. My thoughts collected but I said nothing.

"You broke your word to Lord Marius."

"Yes."

"Why?"

Words cut over my tongue. "Because that blood destroyed everything I loved and held dear."

Lips barely moved in a half-laugh.

"There is nothing precious left in this world now. Nothing save for the blood you destroyed." His face contorted as he growled and lunged for me. Talons plunged into my throat. "You eradicated a chance at evolution for our kind and you speak of love?"

"Love was the only thing worth living for."

He laughed as his talons sunk deeper into my flesh. Blood rushed to the surface.

"So, what do you live for now, hmm?"

He grinned and I stiffened as his gaze trailed to Avila. The scent of my blood spilling over his fingers quickened my pulse. A bright flash pulsed behind my eyes and he was gone just as fast, ensnaring his claws around Avila and hissing.

Bullneck grabbed Sun. She shrieked and pushed against him. He laughed. The sound was hideous. Blade combed a hand through his hair and sniggered. My eyes pierced into Zaros as he gave a drawn-out snarl.

"Perhaps I was wrong." He went to stroke Avila's hair. Her face flushed with resistance, but months of existing from the blood of rodents rendered her useless against his strength. "I never fathered a child, but I do believe the love of a parent is unsurpassed in its power."

Question: *Did I want to find out what happens when a vampire kills one of their own?*

Answer: *Think more on that one. Later.*

I gestured toward Avila and Sun.

"They had no part in discarding the blood. I acted alone."

His eyes blazed. Avila winced as he clutched her tighter.

"And yet, I hear no trace of repentance in your voice." His features dimmed. "Killing one of our own is against clan code. You should know this information if you wish to survive the kindred life. If you survive the kindred life."

Bullneck chuckled.

"Lord Marius wants him alive. The daughter too." Thick fingers stroked Sun's hair. "I want this one."

Sun responded with a sharp elbow and a heated glare. Zaros glared at him.

"Thank you, Athan. Lord Marius wants many things ... but I see him nowhere in this moment, do you?"

"Err ... no."

"Ding, ding!" He laughed and released Avila.

The sense of relief was fleeting as I pulled her closer. His boots barely touched the ground as he began pacing before us.

"Unfortunate accidents have been known to occur in

these tunnels. I for one, am not as forgiving as our Lord Marius." He stopped short of Athan. His face was brutal. "They deserve to die for denying me the opportunity to transcend my powers. Knowing there exists enemy clans out there, do you dare disagree?"

Athan shook his head fast.

"No, sire."

Shit. We're done for.

Zaros turned toward Blade who smirked silently.

"And you?"

"Never, sire. I am with you one hundred percent."

The inky room condensed around me as Zaros grinned before turning back toward me. Ebony skin glistened like slated crystals.

"It is true that Marius senses value in you, but I sense otherwise."

He turned away and sauntered across the room to retrieve a wooden stake propped against the shadowed walls. His features were like stone when he began walking back. He stopped before me and my heart went wild. Avila and Sun gasped as he raised the stake above his head. "I see no use for traitors. There are others that can aid our blood-work endeavors."

He was referring to my hematologist skills, but that was the last thing on my mind right now. I flashed my palms and stepped back.

"Wait!" My words were desperate. "I can help the clan's survival. I have information about the Blood Legend, the prophecy holds true with the birth of the first lineage. Vampires are under threat."

He paused the stake mid-air and regarded me. His voice was a sliver.

"I don't believe you. The Blood Legend prophecy is a myth conjured by the frailty of frantic humans fighting to believe in something when their god failed them."

"You're wrong. Legends and myths are always born from the ashes of truths. The witch in the cells saw it come to pass; she trusts me. I can help destroy the threat."

I didn't know if that woman trusted me, but it was all I had.

My breath stalled as his lips curled into something sinister, but I didn't miss the fear flicker across his eyes. Blade and Athan tittered, and at the same time, the room suddenly erupted with the sounds of other kindred as they came in from the tunnels behind us.

Zaros snorted. He lowered the stake as male and female vampires glided toward the lounge settings. Some of them glanced our way with disinterest. Others grinned and treated us to a mocking wave before settling in to watch the scene unfold. Then his eyes lasered into mine as he leaned closer.

"If I discover you are lying, I will force you to watch while I do unthinkable things to your daughter before I kill you." He pulled back and gave a dismissive wave, flicking his chin toward the guards. "Return them to the cell. We'll continue with this affair later."

I released a breath as he whirled around. He puffed up his chest as he strode toward his clan. Silky hair flipped and lashes fluttered as they greeted him. The burrow filled with sickening croons and sensual murmurs. My stomach lurched. Sun and I exchanged glances. It was repulsion that flooded into me as the guards yanked my arm and pulled me from the lair.

3

IN THE STILL OF THE NIGHT

"Zaros has got it in for you. Clearly, he's defiant in the face of Marius' reign." Sun stopped pacing the cell and spun around. The gravel beneath her boots split in my ear. "He is power hungry. Greedy. I know the look. He's dangerous."

Weariness sunk into my bones. Human waste and rotting rat carcasses drenched my senses. It was rank. I peered up at her from my position on the cell floor.

"He's no more dangerous than Marius."

She shook her head.

"You're wrong. Marius at least is somewhat diplomatic in his thinking. His plans to construct a dome city will grant us freedom to live decently beneath a UV protective canopy. We won't have to be slaves to the night forever. We will know daylight again."

"Not to mention an endless supply of blood," Avila added.

She leaned against the wall. Her eyes shone like sapphires from the shadows. "Marius realizes the importance of humanity. Succumbing to our vampiric urges will eventually result in our demise as the human species dwindles."

Sun grunted.

"Yes, something needs to be done before they become extinct. It's evident who among the kindred leaders has the ability to think ahead." She paused. "There is already dissonance brewing amongst them."

She was right. It was only a matter of time before the new species would fracture into a hierarchy of sorts. We existed in an emerging society. Rules had to be set. Systems needed to be formed. Resistance would inevitably unfold as they vied for power. It would be the most cunning and intelligent vampire who would prevail.

"Zaros is beginning to form his own faction. One of the masters will fall."

I wasn't a big fan of Marius, but after having met Zaros, I knew which side of the fence I'll be landing when the shit hits the fan.

Ah, vampire politics. Let the games begin.

"It's obvious that Zaros allows his primal instincts to influence his decisions," I said.

Avila smirked.

"You give him too much credit. He's just pure asshole, Dad. It is our most undesirable human traits that become accentuated in this condition if we don't learn to tame them."

She shook her head and gestured toward the cell across the way. The hour was late. Human captives slumbered fitfully among the filth and putrid. "Marius speaks of development and normality. He wants to create a blood-letting program. The leftover humans will be sanctioned to live in one half of the city where they can lead a dignified life under Mysticus protection."

Unease rippled through me.

"He told you this?"

"I spent some time with him during the days before we ambushed the hawkers."

The unease deepened to disturbance. She might be a grown woman, but she was still my daughter. I hadn't missed the way Marius had looked at her. I didn't like it. She must have caught my expression because the next thing I heard was her snorting.

"I'm no longer a little girl, Dad." She moved closer and took my hand. Her skin felt like cool rubber. "The world is different now. We're different now. We play by new rules and abide by new kings. Marius is the way toward a peaceful future. He will look after the Leaving humans; give them everything they need. In exchange for their blood, of course."

Of course.

Disbelief. It was a familiar feeling of late. I could hardly fathom my daughter now. The way she spoke of blood and humans as if she had never experienced a mortal life was unnerving. I didn't know if I'd ever get used to it; despite that human blood was now my own weakness. It was an overpowering weakness that repulsed me.

I could barely control it. I didn't know that I even wanted to. My gaze lingered on the human cell. *Irresistible pickings.* Never had human frailty been so acute to me. I groaned inwardly.

"I don't know that Marius' intentions toward the humans are that noble, Avila."

She gave me a squeeze and stood up.

"It's better than living on rodents in a disorganized world with Zaros at the realm." Her voice became grave. "His way would mean a life of squalor and violence."

I grunted a reply as Sun made noises that conveyed her agreement. *Meh.* I could think no longer about smoke-filled bureaucracy and blood-hungry villains. I felt jaded and out of touch. My empty gut cramped.

Blood lust is an insatiable affliction. The energy borrowed from the humans I'd fed on earlier was fast waning. I needed more.

I'm to live out the rest of my days preying on humans.

I should have let Zaros kill me and be done with it. With death came the promise of tranquillity – peace from the torment haunting my soul.

Scarla.

Her pale features danced behind my eyes like a sweet vision. Velvety skin I longed to caress taunted me. I'd give anything to hear her laughter just one more time. *Anything.* But even in death, I knew she'd never forgive me for the brutality of her murder. I was forever damned to the pain of the undead.

I deserved it.

"Dad?"

I looked up at my daughter. I stared back at a replica of someone I loved; someone who would forever appear youthful despite the stretching years ahead. Feelings eluded me. Coldness prevailed. *Can I still love?*

"Yeah?"

"How do you know the witch woman speaks the truth about the prophecy?"

I shrugged.

"Gut feeling."

She was about to respond when the tunnels

suddenly erupted to the sounds of strangled screams and unearthly screeches from the city above. My ears pricked and I stood up. *Instinct overdrive.* My pulse dashed as the disembodied wails clung along the putrid tunnel walls. Sun and I exchanged a look. She frowned.

"What the hell is that?"

I didn't know. It wasn't unusual to hear the occasional scream catch on the night hours. After all, humans were hunted down when the sun sunk on the horizon. But this sounded different. This sounded like the terrified wails of the kindred.

Spectral. Wraithlike. Supernatural.

I didn't utter a word. Clarity evaded me. Avila and I followed Sun as she moved toward the cell bars. We peered out along the dark narrow shaft. The shadows loomed and frolicked in the faint light of candles. Distant water dripped between the walls, broken by the noise of heavy footsteps and harsh shouts; the kindred were on the move.

Urgency.

My hair felt static. Inhuman whines were like sirens and froze my blood. Some of the people in the opposite cell began to stir. But it was when the distinct sound of a lecherous howl filled the dank chamber air that my heart almost exploded.

Avila gasped.

"That was no vampire."

A sudden mass of long-winded screams erupted to reach an ear-piercing peak. They sounded primal. Havoc reigned overhead. Guards yelled at one another. Boots stomped along the sludgy tunnel ground. My stomach flipped as the witch woman caught my eye.

I grasped the steel bars and peered at her as she walked toward the edge of her cell and looked at me. Hair like rusty water almost concealed eyes that glimmered through the space between us. Her lips quivered before forming into an odd grin.

"The lunar is full. The Lygarou have awakened. It has begun."

Sun scowled beside me.

"Stop talking in riddles, woman. What the hell is a Lygarou?"

That was when another hideous howl rang out across the city and seeped through the tunnel walls. It was followed by more shrieks and desperate yells.

My breath stalled and my eyes felt like steel when I looked at the woman. When I spoke, my voice was unrecognizable.

"Answer the question, witch. What is a Lygarou?"

She laughed spontaneously. Grotty fingers clutched the cells bars as she pressed her forehead against the flaking steel poles. She licked her lips and stared heavenward.

"They are wolves born from the sorcery of another era. They are the reason you are what you are; and they will be the death of every vampire and human on earth, including you."

Wolves?

Absurdity.

Sun and Avila gasped in unison. A snarl reverberated. Shrieks like distorted chimes reverberated in my veins. The woman laughed again. *Hysteria.* Suddenly, my body felt numb. Her next words were delivered on the wake of a scream.

"The wolf mother has ignited the Legends of Blood with the birth of her baby. But the power is too raw. The legend genes must mature through the bloodlines. The earth will turn to death once more if the legend isn't silenced."

A gnarly growl followed by a shrilling shout erupted. Then there was silence. My heart missed a beat.

4

LYGAROU BEWARE

A nervous vibe hung over the human captives. Wide eyes blinked from caved sockets and dirty skin. They cowered and trembled. Some of them wept uncontrollably while others murmured to themselves while rocking back and forth. I couldn't blame them. The revelation of the existence of yet another supernatural species was perplexing to say the least.

Werewolves.

It was a chilling thought. I sensed that somehow there was a vital link between their emergence and the rise of the clans. The witch had vaguely mentioned as much. I had no doubt that she spoke the truth. My gut feelings never failed me. I urgently needed to discover more before earth and all its occupants perished at the hands of the Lygarou.

I had to get us out of this cell.

The city above had remained eerily quiet. No longer were the tunnels reverberating to the sounds of stomping footsteps and strangled cries. A feeling of isolation was bestowed upon the chambers. We had no way of knowing the outcome of the attack or how many Lygarou had descended on the city. We could be sitting ducks down here. We could be dog food.

All these thoughts circled through my mind when Sun grabbed my elbow. It was horror that I saw brimming in her eyes.

"Wolves that attack and kill vampires? Can things get any more bizarre in this world?"

Ironic words coming from the mouth of a vampire. The notion fizzled as I clenched my teeth and prepared to answer when the witch woman piped up. She stood apart from the others crowding the cell behind her. She appeared calm.

"Not just any wolves; they are of the Lygarou bloodline. The purest of werewolves created by a powerful Demilune French witch named Evanora a long time ago." She paused to brush a lock of hair from her eye. "I believe the modern term for the reawakened is Lystalkers."

"That doesn't sound so comforting." Avila pushed off the wall to face the woman. "How do you know all of this? Who are you?"

"My name is Clio. My ancestry belongs with the Demilune Circle; the buried and secret coven of witches and sorcerers who originated in the mountains. I know all of this because the stories and folklore have passed through the generations." She gave a rueful laugh. "I'd always thought the Legends of Blood and the Lygarou to be fanciful fables conjured by the ancestors to entertain. I was wrong."

Sun snorted.

"Clearly." She shook her head. "Why now?"

"It was etched to unfold the moment one of Evanora's Lygarou defied their peaceful mountain existence to seek a life among the humans. Shane. He was the first created and the reason behind the curse that rendered the species dormant." She swallowed hard and her voice became urgent as the sound of boots trudged along the passage shafts. "The baby has broken the curse and awakened the pack, but the Lystalkers are unaccustomed to their werewolf genes; they're primitive. This new breed has to be stopped."

Guttural bellows spiraled ahead of the guards heading our way. My eyes darted to their shadows stretching along the walls as they rounded the bend. I frowned and leaned forward.

"How do we stop them?"

Clio began stepping back, dousing herself in the gloom among her captives. Her lips barely moved but I heard every word regardless.

"The wolf mother and her child must be destroyed. It's the only way."

Murder a newborn?

I knew that some part of me should have rejected that notion, yet there was no trace of resistance within me. My mind whirled. The guards hollered and sneered at us as they came to a stop in front of the cells, and one of them began rattling the keys to unlock the cell gates.

"Back up, convicts."

It was Blade and Athan, and they were joined with others I didn't recognize. I swallowed a pang of annoyance and moved away from the cell gate. Another rendezvous with Zaros was the last thing I needed to deal with right now. Not with the appearance of the Lystalkers.

Blade grinned as he stepped over the threshold. Despite his smirk, he smelled like fear.

"Lord Marius has requested your presence at once." He barked an order at his cronies, but his eyes never left mine. "Fetch the witch. We're all going on a trip to reckoning."

"Sounds cheerful," I said. "Should we pack light or heavy?"

Yellow eyes glowered.

"Well, look who has a case of the smart-ass. See how that works for you in the immediate future."

We shall indeed.

He tossed his shiny mane in a fast pivot and I looked at my daughter. She stood defiant, glaring and grasping her hips as she watched the guards when they began ushering us from the cell. *My tough little nugget.* Her eyes skimmed to me and I forced a smile. A tinge of affection shimmied through my heart and there it was – love. It still existed in my core. I was grateful.

"Come on, hurry along!" Athan yelled. "We don't have all night; it's almost daybreak."

I braced myself and silently followed them from the cell as they began leading us and Clio from the underground chambers. I focused ahead and tried to still my thoughts. It would be the first time that I'd be in the company of the vampire that had sired me since our capture months before.

He had branded me a traitor, but I knew he wished to keep me and Avila alive. Otherwise, we'd be long dead by now. My experience as a hematologist was the one card up my sleeve – the knowledge I'd acquired during my humanity. Still, there was little trust among the kindred, and I was certain he had a plan of retribution for me.

The night air was warm and stale, but I welcomed every breath as we finally stepped out from the underground passages and into the city streets. I inhaled deeply, savoring the stars hanging between giant glass towers. I took a beat before marching after the guards. *Tangy iron.* It was salty and sweet, and hung all around. My stomach churned with the scent of fresh blood and strewn body parts littering the pavement and roads along the way.

Shivers.

Cold snapped through me. I sought out Avila's hand with my own and gave her a reassuring squeeze. She pressed her palm into mine. Her fear trickled into me.

"It will be okay."

She nodded.

"I won't let anything happen to you."

The words were out before I could catch them. Promises meant nothing anymore. Not in this new world. I'd promised the same thing to Scarla. She was dead. I couldn't fail Avila again. Whatever was coming, one thing that I knew for certain was my belief in my daughter. I would grip that faith with everything I had.

Zaros was right. The love of a parent is all-powerful. Her survival was all that mattered now. Even if that meant the death of a newborn baby and her mother. Even if that meant my own death.

5

THE RECKONING

It's strange how easily we adapt to new concepts and realities when left with no alternative. The fact that I had died to my humanity to embody a creature I'd only ever known as a fictitious character in books and movies should have been a shocking notion, and yet the opposite was true.

I carefully stepped over a severed head laying in a pool of blood on the stairs leading toward the building entrance. Matted hair the color of strawberry clumped across a gaping bloodied jaw and shockingly frightful features. The fading moon cast silvery shadows, distorting bruised lips and hollow eye sockets. I didn't even balk at the sight of it. Death had become customary.

Derangement.

The streets mirrored a garish Halloween scene. Torn flesh and spilled innards were everywhere. My nostrils blazed. It stunk like an abattoir. Not that I'd ever visited one, but I didn't need to in order to make that comparison. This blood-soaked world was enough.

Lystalkers.

It was clear their bygone genetics were underdeveloped upon their rebirth. *Then again, could the jaws of a werewolf ever be anything but savage?* The hairs on my arms rose. Another supernatural species that sought to replace a new reality. I was dealing with it well, all things considered. Not much could surprise me anymore.

Avila shuddered.

"Barbarous creatures. Do they have no finesse?"

We stopped behind the guards as one of them opened the lobby door. I glanced at her.

"Is *there* a sophisticated manner to murder, my dear?"

"Well, yeah. *We* might be killers, but at least we carry out our indiscretions with competence."

My jaw fell.

"Is that what you call it?"

She shrugged but said nothing as Blade ushered us inside the building.

"Hurry up slayers."

I grimaced, barely noticing Athan leer at Sun as I stepped across the threshold. Avila's image flashed in my mind the day I'd first brought her here. She had tried hard to control her terror as she clutched a stake at the lobby doors. It was the same day I had delivered her into the hands of Marius. She was different now. The world was green.

Guilt lingered like moss growing at the bottom of a pond. It was relentless. But this was no time to dwell on a past I couldn't change. It was time to receive Blade's promised reckoning. This was apparent when I spotted Marius striding across the lobby toward us.

Clio gasped but I didn't look at her. My eyes were glued on Marius. He appeared like a cinematic vision and moved with formidable force. It was clear that he was pissed. I began to suspect that his reckoning might be about to take on a whole new meaning. I tried to keep calm as he stopped short of me.

"So, here you are. The one I entrusted to return to me what I most seek."

His black hair was slicked across his scalp to accentuate dark penetrating eyes and his sallow complexion highlighted thick ruby lips.

The guards shrunk back. Sun and Avila were either side of me with Clio behind as we stood near the lobby door.

"Marius."

The lobby felt dreary and desolate. Murky corridors ran off into darkness and a chill hung in the air despite the heat outside. A sofa marked the center of the room, and scantily dressed women moaned softly as they draped themselves across lounges. Their heads lolled.

Humans.

I felt a rush through my veins, but the sound of Marius' brash tone quickly quelled the taunting hunger. I steadied my gaze back on him.

"I trust you've enjoyed your time with the cockroaches and sewer rats these past months?"

The guards sniggered and Avila scowled. She shrunk closer to me when Marius gave a black grin. His eyes settled on her.

"I expected more from you, Livvy." He reached to stroke her chin.

Livvy?

My thoughts whirled and I almost missed the flicker in her eyes as she gazed at him. *Since when did this happen?* My blood felt like mercury. Marius cackled.

"Still, I don't suppose that you would be disloyal to your father. Love can be a powerful force that drives us to carry out the unthinkable – like discard rare blood – that had you kept your promise, would have been extremely useful considering the threat of what we are now facing." He glared at me. "Do you have anything to say?"

"There is nothing I can say that will change what I've done, but *Livvy* and Sun were not involved in the decision to destroy the blood. It was all me." I shook my head. "Whatever plans you have by way of retribution, leave them out of it. They've suffered enough."

"And because of your decisions, we're all suffering now!" He growled and stepped closer. I could almost taste the fresh blood on his breath. "I lost at least two dozen vampires tonight to a pack of flea-bitten mongrels and you speak of suffering?"

I kept silent and tried not to focus on the inflamed blood vessels at his temples.

"I expect nothing but loyalty from those I have sired. Have you forgotten the gift I readily bestowed on you when you turned up practically begging for eternal life? Do you have no gratitude for all that I've done for you and your family?"

The guards grunted in agreement. I ignored them.

Gratitude?

I almost choked.

Clearly, this vampire had a selective memory. It was he who had destroyed my family.

I bit back words and reined in my thoughts before he

could collect either of them. My voice was much more even than I'd anticipated.

"I accept that I am now kindred and a member of the Mysticus clan, and I will honor my position as such."

Fact: *I had no choice at this point.*

He gave a half laugh and moved back, peering beyond me to Clio.

"You shall indeed. If you want those that remain precious to you to keep breathing, that is. It is time that your loyalty is renewed through acts of demonstration and service to the clan." His fangs glistened like pearls. "The witch woman knows secrets about the dogs?"

"Yes."

"I'm listening."

I glanced at Clio. Her dark eyes looked wild.

"The birth of a baby has broken a curse and awakened the Lygarou blood genes. Those reawakened are feral in their transformation and are unable to control their natural instincts." I shook my head. "Apparently, the only way to destroy them all is to kill the child and her mother. I don't know the details surrounding the curse or the sorcerer who originally created the Lygarou, but I do know that the species is somehow linked to the origins of the Vampiric virus and I'd like to consult with Michal on this subject."

"Why?"

"Because knowledge is power."

Black eyes gleamed like metallic paint.

"Agreeable. Your scientific skills are an asset to the clan that I will need when the creation of the dome city is completed – Bloodfaye will provide us protection from enemy clans and ..." His lips curled. "The wolves. Ascension for us, if you will. We shall live a dignified future where we will co-exist with the humans. After all, we cannot afford to behave bestial if we are to thrive as the dominant species. I need those who can think beyond their bloodthirst. Given your educational background, I sense that you are more than capable to adopt a grow mindset. Am I correct?"

I was about to answer when a voice bellowed from someplace deep within a corridor cavity. It was familiar. *Zaros.* An instant ache sprung in my head.

"Ha! A grow mindset would not have so easily destroyed the blood capable of defeating the Lystalkers!"

His boots squished on the tiled floor as he emerged from the shadows. Long, black trench coat tails flowed behind him. I didn't miss Marius' grimace as Zaros came to a stop beside him and glared. "I'm not convinced this vampire has the clan's best interests at heart. Even in his undead affliction, he remains romantic."

Marius didn't even look at him.

"Whether you realize it or not, Zaros, it is the

undead heart that remembers his humanity that will further the clan into evolution. Perhaps this is something worth pondering on your part."

Zaros snorted.

"We are different creatures now. Romantic hearts are a sign of weakness that belongs in the days past, as is our humanity." He paused to glance at Athan and Blade. They stifled sniggers and Zaros grinned. "What of soft-cock's punishment?"

Marius and Zaros glared at each other for several tense moments. Sun and I exchanged glances. Marius licked his lips and looked at me.

"Some of us are still learning the vital qualities required in order to solidify the clan's future survival," Marius said. He ignored Zaros' loud snort. "I will grant you access to Michal and the lab on the condition that you take the witch, a few of my men and hunt down that wolf-mother and her baby."

My thoughts began to reel.

"You will not return to the city until you have killed them both."

Sun stood defiantly with hands on hips.

"Are you crazy? The wolf-mother and her baby are hidden some place in the mountains and probably heavily guarded. It's too dangerous for any Mysticus vampire to venture that far from the city, let alone face a pack of wolves on unfamiliar territory. The journey will take days. How are we supposed to shelter from the sunlight? What if we are ambushed?"

Marius laughed.

"Tsk, Tsk. You have it all muddled up in your sweet little head. You little vampire ladies will be staying here with me as leverage. If he fails or attempts to flee the clan, I will slaughter the both of you."

Zaros began laughing. I cringed.

"Perfect! Let's see how the sob story handles the big bad new world." He leered at Avila. "I daresay daddy will be the death of you yet."

I wanted to murder him.

6

WITH THE WIND

"Haaa!" Michal screeched. He rounded the laboratory bench and scurried closer. He stopped abruptly when he got a good look at me. His face paled beneath layers of filth. Grotty fingers knotted franticly. "Ya ... you're a vampire?"

I barely nodded. His freckled eyes skirted the floor.

"You were supposed to get the blood out of the city; you were the one I chose to protect it."

"I got it out of the city."

His gaze darted owl-like through clouded spectacles. His voice was tremulous.

"Then where is it? Is it safe?"

"It's gone."

His mouth formed a huge "O".

"Gone?"

"With the wind."

I pushed past him, striding further into the lab and scanning the area. Not much had changed since my last visit. The lighting was dim, and it was cold, and it still reeked of human waste and rotting flesh. However, a glance into the killing room cubicle revealed no mangled bodies this time around.

Repulsion.

It was overpowering. His feet sounded like a mini stampede as he trotted after me. When I stopped and turned around to face him, he almost collided into my chest. I moved away, stretching the distance between us while vaguely wondering how any vampire could desire his blood.

I wouldn't feed on him if he were the last human on earth.

In the next instant, he was hiking up sleeves that knew better days and thrusting his wrists toward me. Beady eyes popped.

"For you, Master."

"Huh?" I grimaced. "No."

Lord no.

"Why? I wish to serve you."

I forced a part smile.

"Marius keeps me well fed, thank you."

It was true. Days had passed since forming our

agreement. Well, if you call it that. We had been promptly moved from the cells and into more pleasant living conditions where hot showers and human blood were freely available.

It is amazing how fear can drive us. Marius was beside himself with the threat of the Lystalkers attacking again on the next moon. He was certain they were gathering in numbers during their dormancy stage. That they sought to form a strong outbreak against the clan.

I agreed.

The next series of attacks will prove more dire if we didn't do something to protect ourselves. It was an ironic twist that we were no longer at the top of the food chain. What Marius had not realized was that he needn't have used my daughter as leverage in order to gain my assistance. I would do anything to make sure she stayed safe. *Anything.*

The stakes were higher now because I had no choice but to kill that baby and her mother or it meant Avila's death. I couldn't allow that to happen. I'd already lost her once to the kindred.

However, other matters dominated my thoughts right now – matters of government secrets, blood and viruses. I watched Michal as he hunched and shifted awkwardly, his eyes steadying on his boots as he spoke.

"No more AB positive blood type means no way to

study its astonishing effects on those infected by the virus. It could've been the path to finding a cure."

"I think it would've empowered ego-driven vampires and caused much more destruction before a cure could have been cultivated. There is no way you could have worked the blood here with their knowledge. You know that; that's why you gave it to me."

He rubbed a palm over his balding scalp. Sweat glistened.

"Tell me about Shane."

He jerked suddenly. He lifted his eyes toward the roof and froze before swallowing hard.

"Sha ... Shane?"

"Did I stutter?"

"N ... no, no, Master." He shook his head furiously. "How do you know about Shane? That was confidential information that very few had access to."

"Call it a hunch."

It was the truth. I mean, it didn't take much to make the link, what with Clio mentioning the connection between vampires and Lygarou. Then Shane seeking a life among humans.

"Huh. Nice hunch."

"Yeah, now talk. What is the connection between the V-Virus and the Lygarou?"

He chewed on his bottom lip and shook his head.

"Makes no difference now. Shane was special. I don't know how the agency discovered the gifts in his blood; he was already here when I was recruited. He told me they hunted him down for years before his capture. He told me that he was the first werewolf; the alpha."

"He became their guinea pig."

He nodded. "More than that, he became the crux of a series of biological experiments. His blood was unbelievable! I'd never seen anything like it." His voice pitched and he blinked rapidly. "The rate at which his blood cells regenerated was phenomenal; his white cells were abnormal, and his iron levels should've rendered him dead."

"What happened?"

He laughed.

"The V-Virus was born, that's what happened. It all went to shit."

"Yeah, no shit." My fangs began to ache. "Where is he now?"

Michal shrugged. His next words hit hard.

"He escaped not long after the virus took hold, but not before vowing to destroy every one of us."

"So, he pro-created to unlock the curse and awaken the Lystalkers."

"Exactly."

Terrific.

Turns out we have an alfa wolf with a vendetta on our hands. *Could things get any worse?* I shuddered to think but think I must. My thoughts unraveled as I spun on my heels and began pacing. Talons combed through my dark hair, and I was aware of Michal's fixed stare.

"The witch woman who knows about the Lygarou says the baby carries the Blood Legend gene, whatever that means. What if I can get a sample of her blood?"

His brows rose. "Her blood could be the pathway toward finding a cure for the virus. It could be the missing link that eluded us all along!"

I strode up to him and gripped his collar. He shrieked and whimpered as I twisted the fabric between my talons.

"I'll bring back the blood of the baby, but you had better keep those flappy gums of yours closed or I'll remove your heart from your chest with my palm. Do you understand?"

He nodded fast. "Yes, Master!"

I could feel my veins bulging at my throat. "Good." I released him and stepped away, throwing my next words over my shoulder as I walked from the lab. "And don't call me 'Master'."

7

BLOOD BATH ON THE HORIZON

Motionless air clung to my skin with the balmy night and half-moon. It was comforting. I couldn't get warm enough. No amount of natural heat could thaw my cold blood.

What am I? I was neither alive nor dead. *Limbo.* I lingered some place in the in-between. Perhaps it was hell on earth. Happiness was a memory, and an emotion I never expected to feel again. Still, the warm night air was the closest I could get to feeling normal.

The tree leaves bristled slightly. *Bats.* They were abundant and appeared to follow our movements through the dense forest grounds. Night creatures hunted. The sound of a long howl broke in the distance.

"Wha ... what was that?" Clio said.

She smelled like wild daisy.

"Obviously it was a wolf."

The snappy reply was delivered by Lena. She was one of the two Shadow Guardians who accompanied us on the quest to hunt the wolf-baby. She was a tough middle-aged Latino woman with braided yellow hair and black roots. Her skin appeared like overused leather and her legs went on forever.

Clio scowled.

"Yes, but was it ..." Her voice trailed and I glanced at her. Glossy red curls accentuated the dark eyes peering back at me. They'd cleaned her up. Even given her fresh clothes. There were perks to being a witch with valued knowledge. You got the treatment.

She gave a nervous laugh. "Na ... it's not a full moon. It's their cousins. I bet they sense their alpha's rebirth."

Lena snorted. I felt irritated. She wasn't the most pleasant human. Her attitude sucked harder than a newborn vampire.

"How do you know all this shit about the Lystalkers?"

She grabbed Clio's elbow suddenly and yanked hard, causing Clio to stumble back. The earth crunched as she shrieked and fell against Lena's chest. I stopped walking and whirled around as Lena spat her next words in Clio's face.

"Are you some kind of freaky sorcerer leading us into a trap?"

Clio wriggled her arm against Lena's grip. Her eyes blazed.

"Let go of me, wench!"

Lena grinned. She flicked opened a blade with her other hand and pointed it toward Clio's throat. Her elongated neck gleamed as she bent forward and sneered.

"What if I let you go in pieces, witch-bitch?"

I groaned inwardly.

Humans. Have they not experienced enough violence?

Clio balled her fist along with her face. I saw the oncoming actions long before the sequence could play out. It was time to intervene. My feet barely touched the ground as I slid between them, snatching the blade from Lena's grasp and growling in her face.

"Leave the woman be."

She shrunk away as the rest of our group closed in around us. It was Blade and Athan, and the other Shadow Guardian whose name was Hugo. He resembled a cross between Bob Marley and a fart. His personality was like moldy cheese. So was his breath as it vapored in my face.

"Let it go, Jett."

I turned on him with a hiss. Blade and Athan laughed. Adrenaline surged. *Hunger.* It was hard not to think about it and Lena just spiked my radar. I was edgy. We'd been hiking for two nights without a decent feed, albeit for the small amounts of blood offered by the Guardians.

Clio and her blood were off limits. I'd made that clear at the onset. Not that she was offering. For some reason, I felt compelled to protect her. At least until we made it to the wolf-mother's den.

Hugo stood in all his graceless glory. Putrid dreadlocks spilled over his shoulders and glued against a spotted brow. His lips looked like deflated tires and one eye twitched franticly.

I took an even breath. My talons itched.

"Keep her leashed, brute."

He nodded. Lena scoffed but I ignored her as I tossed the blade at her feet. Hugo understood. It was enough. I was fast learning their language.

Clio shuffled closer to me. She said nothing but her eyes spoke volumes. Her mind too when I tuned in hard enough. But I couldn't focus that hard right now. I needed blood. She said we'd arrive at our destination the following night. I knew I'd need to replenish before facing whatever awaited us in those mountains.

All of them looked at me. Expectation was apparent. Somehow, this little circus quest had become mine.

"There is only about three hours left until dawn. I know of a small settlement at the foot of the mountains near the river. We can shelter there."

I was about to stalk away when the faint sound of voices drifted through the twisted tree trunks.

I instantly froze to the spot. My eyes trailed back to Blade and Athan. *Excitement.* It had a destiny of its own – a path difficult to ignore. I closed my eyes and tilted my head, sniffing out the sweet claret afforded by bottom-feeder rabble camping in the woods.

Foolish humans.

"Hawkers." My lips hardly moved. "I can smell them a mile away."

"Only hawkers would be stupid enough to be out in the woods after sundown." Blade grinned with elation. "In the mood for a dirty feast?"

Hell yeah.

"Beggars can't be choosers." I looked at Hugo and motioned toward Clio. "Don't take your eyes off her."

I didn't wait for his reply. Saliva formed in my mouth as I anticipated the rush of a feed. It drove me forward. I was a ghoul. *Heinous.* Not even inhuman.

Athan and Blade were velocity. The three of us moved

like force. The night ignited. I saw everything and nothing at the same time as we flew through the forest. Discreet gruntles, subdued laughter and stale whiskey led the way.

We slowed when the clearing came into view and we lingered in the shadows. Athan and Blade stood either side of me as we peered past the trees to survey the scene.

It was a tidy mob of hawkers. Three small tents were pitched at even intervals. Muted light glowed from within worn canvas. Their shadows stretched like a taunting dream. I groaned. A few men sat between the tents drinking ale and smoking pipes.

"There be a rumor running rife about striking a deal with the vamps. I heard tell that they will offer us protection if we agree to give them blood. It might be in our favor to concede what with the state of the new threats."

A big hawker with a wiry beard spluttered. He took a swig of ale.

"Screw that shit. The vamps are as trustworthy as them snotty smush kittens who think they're too good for what we've got packing. Me and Brad made a deal with one of them hoes last night; didn't go as planned."

Laughter erupted.

"What happened?"

"I wanted to eat her out. Show her some tenderness.

She turned me into a vampire. She got the bloody dick instead. The bitch got it hard!"

More laughter followed but I didn't really hear it. My boots felt heavy as I was catapulted back in time. *Scarla.* Her name was a sigh on my tongue. It was hawkers like these that had raped, tortured and murdered her. My heart shattered. Her image filled my mind and I was lost.

Secret amber smiles.

"Dance with me."

Sweet laughter.

"I'm an awful dancer."

Lingering glances and soft skin.

"You're wrong. Your soul dances with mine every day."

Twisted memories and yearning tore at my soul. She had been my Yin; my everything. They took her from me. The pain never stopped. I could never get used to her absence from my life. Black hate twisted through me. The next thing I heard was Blade.

"Bon appetit!"

I looked at him and smiled. The moment was nothing and everything as it bore new revelations. *Truth.* I slipped from the trees and bolted toward them.

I was a vampire.

8

BLOOD LOVER

I breathed deep and stretched my neck back, catching sight of an owl perched among the branches above. The darkness was no barrier as large eyes peered at me from a flat face. I was gorged and reborn with the sanguine liquid flowing through me. I grinned and wiped the blood from my chin with the back of a hand.

"Hello my feathered friend."

My image flashed in his yellow eyes. A stranger peered back at me. The blues of my eyes appeared animated and unnatural against my dark hair. *Incubus.* The thought stole my grin and everything around me dissolved along with the occasional whimper and shriek offered by the surviving hawkers.

The owl knew acts of bestiality and cold murder. I

looked away. It almost felt like God was peering at me through those eyes. Another helping of guilt was the last thing I needed right now. Not that I was feeling ashamed. My father used to say that life was too short to live with guilt and regret. Now, life spread before me like an endless black tarmac. I had plenty of time to wallow in guilt and regret if I so wished. Tonight, I would do away with such notions and be who I was reborn to be – a killer.

Feathered friends be damned.

I gave a half laugh. Euphoria was seduction. Blood my victory. I felt more alive than I had in months, and I couldn't help but respect the unbridled beast within me. *Supernatural energy*. It was disturbingly empowering, and I was fast becoming hooked.

Speaking of beasts, it was Athan's colossal figure that caught my vision as he released a dead male hawker and stood up. His face gleamed the color of red wine and his eyes were inky torpedoes. *Blood-drunk*. He was as delirious as I. He grinned.

"Jett the owl whisperer."

"Ha! Screw the owl. He's too uptight up there on his squeaky clean, high-horse branch."

He laughed and picked up a stone.

"Fucking owl, like *he* doesn't kill to survive."

I had hardly registered that he had pitched the

stone when I heard a dull thump as the owl landed at my feet. I looked down at it and grimaced. It was as dead as the hawker Athan had just drained and dumped.

Goodbye feathered friend.

Athan laughed as Blade's throaty cackle broke out ahead of him as he strode toward us. He stopped short of me and slapped me on the shoulder.

"Looks like the soft-cock just got himself a hard-on!"

Athan laughed.

"Yeah, he's evolving alright. I'm not sure which Master will be more pleased."

Blade licked blood from his lips. Lemon eyes were ablaze.

"Hmm ... let me see ... the one with the vision, or the one with the vision?"

They broke into laughter, but I ignored them as I looked around. Mortality and oblivion hung heavy in the balmy night air. The scene appeared as if straight out of a Dracula movie. Corpses and torn flesh were strewn all around while evidence of blood was splattered across the earth and the tents.

Hmm ...

Apparently, some vampires relished the kill more than others and took pleasure in shredding their victims before draining them. Avila would be affronted. Oddly enough, I looked forward to filling her in when I returned to the city.

My gaze settled on the small cluster of hawkers huddled against a flimsy tent canvas. I counted two men, one woman and a child. They dared not move as they sniveled beneath wild stares. My attention settled on the boy who looked to be about ten years old. I could smell his tender blood from here. Thoughts vanished as I fixed my stare on him.

Desire. My heart thumped as my senses spiked. Dark velvety eyes brimmed and peered back at me as he curled into his mother's chest. A lock of brown hair fell over one brow while rosebud lips pouted, and his pulse became my rhythm.

Remarkably, I felt famished again. My nostrils fired up and I began to move forward, led by the promise of young blood. It was thrilling. *Impelling even.* Resistance was unattainable until Blade grabbed my arm and shattered my trance. His voice boomed.

"Taking children is forbidden, greenhorn. It's against clan code."

My eyes flashed as I fought to contain vigorous impulses. Including the dumbest response ever.

"Why?"

"Because we have to conserve our future blood supply, that's why." He laughed. "Hell, even Zaros adheres to this code despite that the blood of the young is the most difficult to resist."

Athan smirked.

"Yeah, children's blood is what caviar and white truffle used to be to the rich folk. It's a delicacy denied to us, so learn to control yourself, slayer, or you'll find yourself burning to a crisp come dawn."

It was the longest statement I'd heard him utter thus far. I remained silent. *What was I thinking?* Self-disgust erupted as I looked back at the child, and it was a question I knew I would ask myself repeatedly over the coming days. It was also one I couldn't answer.

I barely knew myself anymore. I felt like a modern-day Dr Jekyll, however my alter ego was more terrifying than a psychotic serial killer who liked to slice up hookers for pleasure.

The supernatural powers and urges that accompanied vampirism were overwhelming, particularly when confronted by blood and insatiable hunger. I knew that I would have to learn to be a vampire without allowing the beast within control me, at least not all the time.

That was much easier said than done. I was discovering rather quickly how easy it was to succumb to ruthlessness and apathy because it was now my second nature. Marius was right; it was those rare vampires who held onto empathy that were needed if we were to have any kind of future, and not only to preserve our blood supply. I sensed something much more profound at play here.

Philosophical thoughts took a backseat when I caught sight of a figure dashing from one of the tents. A whirring vision of scarlet fabric and long dark tresses disappeared into the woods. *A woman.* My pulse quickened. Blade and Athan laughed, and their banter followed me as I instantly took off after her.

"Ha, would ya look at that!"

"She's got more balls than a juggling circus act."

"Go on, slayer – go get your wild cat!"

I tuned out their chortles as I entered the dense vegetation. I became still, closing my eyes to focus on her. *Ba-bump. Ba-bump.* Her heart was a melody that merged with the forest sounds and set me in motion. My breath was shallow. The earth didn't even feel me as I weaved through the twisted trunks like a firebolt.

She stopped running and I immediately paused. My eyes darted over wild bramble and vivid ferns as I searched her out. A twig snapped followed by a gasp. I licked my lips and whirled toward the sound as she began running again. A flash of red blinded my vision. She veered around a tree. I grinned and leapt forward. She couldn't outrun me.

The wooded air condensed around me. Her feet crushed timberland turf, dragging over fronds and leaves just ahead of me. I slowed and rounded a trunk to see her grasping a branch and heaving. Black dewy eyes shone like a starless night sky beneath pitch hair. Her lips quivered like crushed cherries on creamy skin. She looked to be about Avila's age, maybe a little older, and she was flawless.

I drummed my talons against a trunk.

"Are you done running?"

She squared her chin; eyes reduced to slits. My gaze fell to the rise of her full breasts straining against flimsy fabric. Her skirt swirled at her feet. She carried the faint scent of musk. I was captivated.

"I ... I guess I am." She struck out her hips and clasped them. Her eyes glimmered. "What are you going to do?"

"I'm going to kill you."

She inhaled sharply, and her eyes never left mine.

"Do what you must, vampire."

Arousal overload.

"Thank you, madam."

She didn't flinch when I walked closer and roughly grabbed the back of her skull. Her hair felt silky for a hawker woman. But I didn't dwell on that for any longer than necessary. Her blood screamed my name. I tilted her head so that the skin of her throat revealed itself to me. *Glory.* Blue veins stretched like wonderous candy. I couldn't stop even if I wanted to. I didn't want to.

Her heart raced as I gripped her hair and curled back my lips to sink my fangs into flesh that revealed sweet offerings.

Blood Lover.

It was all I could think as the moment claimed me. A whimper reverberated into my ear. Her pulse throbbed like a lilting symphony as I siphoned her blood and relished the warmth as it filled my mouth and made me whole again. Ecstasy found me.

Was this my heaven on earth now?

Then suddenly:

"Jett – no, stop!"

Hands clawed at my back and small fists pounded my arm.

What the hell?

The woman slumped against me as I turned with a fierce growl to catch Clio's wild eyes glaring at me. Blood dripped over my chin and my hiss deepened, but it didn't seem to faze her. Instead, she shook her head and scowled, before she went to the woman.

"She's only a young woman and you've just about killed her!" Her lips pulled tight. "You can't kill this one, Jett. Do you understand?"

Understand? Now there's an interesting word for a world where very little made sense these days. I looked at the woman who I still held in my arms. She appeared lifeless. My voice was unrecognizable.

"It may be too late."

9

PURE HEART

"This wasn't part of the plan."

Lena wrenched the curtains closed. Brass on brass chinked into my ears as she turned to glare at whoever was listening. Unfortunately, her abrasive voice was difficult to ignore.

I leaned back into the armchair and regarded her. It was overstuffed and stunk like old mac-and-cheese, but that was the least of my concerns.

"Welcome to the discovery plan."

The others laughed. Lena didn't. Her dark eyes turned to slivers.

"This is the witch's doing. It's all going to shit, what with babysitting these hawkers. I don't like it and I don't trust her."

A tiny weathered wood cabin plus one witch, two

Guardians, three vampires, an almost dead woman and hawker prisoners made for one brutal headache.

Not to mention the state of the shack. It was crammed with timeworn furniture over filthy rugs that barely covered the gaping cracks in the floorboards.

At least there was light. *Bonus.* Whoever dwelled here in the past had possessed a fetish for oil lanterns.

I pushed my hair back. Weariness radiated in my bones.

"Trust is overrated in the new world. You will do as instructed and leave for the city with the mother and child at first light."

Grotty fingers dug at her hips. She held my stare for a few tense moments before looking away.

"Very well," she said. "The windows will need thicker coverings if you are to slumber here for the day. I'll see about fetching blankets."

I gave a curt nod as she stalked from the room. She made no attempt to disguise her frustration.

This was made more evident when the sounds of cupboard doors being slammed and banged was heard from other parts of the shack.

It was Hugo I heard next.

"Heh. She's going at it like killing snakes!"

He lingered awkwardly by the threshold of the room where we had stowed the surviving hawkers. His broad shoulders hunched below a chronic eye twitch as he laughed. He looked like pig on ice.

I ignored him. My mind was a whirlwind. We hadn't quite made it to the town at the foot of the mountains. Instead, we were holed up in a half-rotted cabin that Clio had found. Our friendly local witch was full of surprises.

Perhaps she wasn't as far removed from her genetic origins as she had made out. Blade brought me back to the present with his clucky mouth.

"She does have a point. What of this discovery plan – couldn't we just let the woman die and leave the mother and child to their own devices and carry on?"

I wanted to roll my eyes. *Did nobody pay attention?*

"We could but we're not. The child's blood and his mother will be safer in the city. I think the masters would agree considering we're talking *delicacy* blood. We can afford to continue one man short."

"How can you be so sure?"

I shrugged.

"Wolves remain in their human form between moons. I'm certain we can overcome them easily enough provided we arrive before the next lunar."

Lemon eyes squinted. "You're certain of this?"

"I've seen *The Wolfman*, I know how it goes."

His brows raised but he said nothing more as Lena

returned with an armful of blankets. Her nose scrunched with the flick of her braid.

"They reek of mothballs and rat shit."

I grinned.

"That's the least of your problems."

She snorted as she set about draping the bedding over the windows; an act that instantly strangled the already constricted space. Her mouth offered a running dialog.

"I watched *The Wolfman* once at my aunt's place. She lived on the Northern Fringes. I was just a little girl. Thought she was the coolest adult until I couldn't sleep for a week."

Athan cackled. His massive figure almost concealed the sofa.

"You mean you weren't always a tough bitch? Hard to wrap my head around that one."

She whirled around to face him, delivering her words through gritted teeth.

"Wrap your big head around this, vampire. I saw those wolves with my own eyes when they attacked the city. They make *The Wolfman* seem like Scooby-Doo." She looked at me. "You best pray that you're right; those wolves were more savage than any vampire I've seen."

"I don't pray."

They continued exchanging remarks, but I tuned out

for the most part. Talk of savage wolves turned my thoughts to Avila and Sun. They were safe for now and I needed to keep it that way.

The truth was, I didn't know crap about the wolves and how their shifter phase worked, but it was obvious the moon cycle was involved. Otherwise, we'd all be dog meat by now.

As it was, there was about five nights before the next full moon.

Time is of the essence.

I tried to relax in the knowledge that we had plenty of time to get to the wolf mother's den, slaughter some canine and get out before they had a chance to transform into heinous gobblers. After that, it was happy days. No more wolf problem and no more threat on my daughter's life.

I did have to find a discreet moment to steal a bit of the puppy's blood via the syringe I carried before I killed her. No way could the others get wind of that little side angle. It was too important.

Who knew what treasures the blood of this baby held?

I was curious as to what secrets her blood may unlock, if at all. I could only hope that it may provide a pathway into discovering a cure for the V-virus, or at least give us something to hope for.

Imagine a world without werewolves and vampires? That would be a world in which I would pray.

All these musings were lost at the sudden ear-piercing shrill that echoed along the shack's short hallway. It was Clio. She had opted to stay with the wounded woman who lay on a thin cot in one of the rooms.

I didn't react immediately but my stomach did clench when she called out my name. Trepidation rose as I stood up and made for the room.

Honestly, *wounded* may not have been the most appropriate choice of words to describe the woman's condition. I mean, she was literally drained of blood.

Does that count as wounded? Stupid question, Jett.

But stupid is, is stupid does and the world is now full of stupid questions; like the fact that Clio had stopped me from completing the kill and then had us haul the woman to this dump for a start. I didn't like it, yet something compelled me to take heed of the witch's words.

Discomfort would have to take a backseat. Time for the big-boy pants. Although, as soon as I got wind of Clio's next words, those pants weren't feeling so great.

She knelt beside the cot where the woman lay as still as a coffin. Clio's knuckles whitened over the woman's flaccid hand while a shock of her red hair almost buried the woman's face as she whispered in her ear.

"Hold on, Bella donna. Hold on."

I froze. My talons sunk into the timber threshold. *Bella donna.* They were the same words I had often used for Scarla. My heart squeezed and Clio looked up at me. Her eyes were wide.

"Jett! Hurry!"

I frowned as my gaze fell to the woman. Her black hair was a striking contrast against a pale pillow and the blue tinging her lips. Thick lashes appeared like bottlebrush. Comprehension eluded me. I shook my head.

"What?"

She stood up and marched toward me. She gripped my hand and pulled. "You need to make her kindred now. We need the blood of a newborn vampire."

"Huh? No!"

"You must, Jett!" She tightened her fingers around mine. "It's the only way to protect any hope of reviving humanity in the future."

I couldn't think.

"What? Why?" I snatched my hand away. "Why me?"

Her voice lowered. "Because it was you who discarded the transcendental blood and kept me alive.

You are the one; the pure heart that remains in vampire form. You are a vital part of conserving the prophecy." She gestured toward the woman. "As is she."

Tingles spread along my spine and my pure heart almost stopped.

10

I SOLD MY SOUL AGAIN

Madness. I had been drawn into a world I didn't want. My insides churned with all kinds of protests as I sat leaning against the wall in the corner of the room. I longed for the rotting floorboards to swallow me whole. Oblivion was an enticing affliction, and yet it eluded me just as the sun remained evasive.

What did I just do?

There was no way back now. I had done the unthinkable. Clio said that my heart was pure and that my presence and participation was important to the prophecy. *Strain.* Everything racked on the inside. I gripped my skull. The taste of my own blood was fresh on my lips. I could hardly fathom the reality. If indeed my heart was as pure as what she had said, then it was no longer. I had just crossed a threshold with no option to return – I had sired another, and in the process, I sold my soul again.

"You've done the right thing." Clio sat down next to me. She pushed a lock of hair from her eyes and smiled. "Thank you."

Shouldn't the right thing feel right?

"For what, exactly?" I motioned toward the woman who had fed off my blood. She was motionless. Dead. "She didn't ask for this life. I'm a fiend."

"You're wrong, she asked when she told you to do what you must. In that final moment, she didn't resist your vampire bite."

"I didn't interpret that as a request to become kindred, Clio."

I rubbed my wrist where the puncture marks were fast healing. I could still feel the sensation of her sucking the blood from my veins. It had felt critical.

She frowned. "We can't always see through the blur in front of us. This world has become an altered reality of the past. The same rules don't apply; everything has changed. We must cultivate and use our higher senses to help guide the way back."

I swung my gaze to my boots and studied the dried earth that clung around the edges. My father used to say that we couldn't control how the world and people changed, we could only manage our response to it. He said those were the qualities that defined us. I felt defined alright and I couldn't say I was digging it.

Still, perhaps this was why I felt compelled to trust her. She was like a rainbow in a blackened world. Still, I needed more than just an abstract anecdote. My breath felt like glass when I looked at her.

"Back to what? You mentioned the woman was vital in reviving humanity, but how?"

She gave a rueful laugh. "My grandmother was one of the last practicing Demilune Sisters. As a child she would take me up into the mountains where she spent time honoring the ancestors and brewing magical potions. I'd help her collect wild berries and rare herbs like blueleaf and darknut. Those days seem like a dream now." She paused and her eyes glazed. "She used to tell me that I was special, and that someday my gifts would reveal themselves at a time when the earth turned to darkness. I never believed her ... until the V-virus took hold and activated something within me."

"Your gifts?"

"Yes." Her eyes narrowed. "I ... I don't even know myself anymore. These feelings and visions wash over me like messages from an invisible realm ... a higher place or something. I have to trust it. I'd like you to trust it too."

"Your grandmother was right, Clio. You are special. Whoever you're becoming in this new world, don't allow the evil to steal your light."

She reached out and stroked the back of my hand. Her skin felt warm. Longing swelled.

"I don't have the answers. I'm not exactly sure of her role yet, but I do have faith. Do you, Jett?"

Ha. Faith was a blind resolve based on nothing but an unfaltering belief you find true, good and beautiful. *Scarla.* My faith in the love I had for her had propelled me into greater states of appreciation during our time together. She made me want to be a better man. Of course, that was before the apocalypse, and faith didn't prevent her death.

The woman stole my thoughts and attention as she began to stir. She groaned softly. I stood up and looked at Clio as she stretched to her feet beside me.

"Why did you call her 'Bella donna' earlier?"

Her shoulders slumped in a half shrug.

"I'm not sure. Why?"

"No reason."

She was about to say something when the woman groaned louder and sat up suddenly. She blinked repeatedly beneath a dark wide stare that settled on us. Her features were a milky compilation of sharp cheekbones, a petite nose and full lips that slackened.

She was obviously perplexed, but she was striking nonetheless.

Clio rushed to her bedside.

"Hello, Bella donna. How do you feel?" Her gesture to stroke a strand of hair from the woman's face was met by a fast hiss as she shrunk back. Clio faltered. "I'm not going to hurt you."

The woman's eyes shaded and her chest heaved as she regarded Clio. I knew the look. Hunger. It was ravenous upon reawakening as the undead, and her sights were firmly set on Clio.

Crap.

My nerves shot through me and we moved at the same time. The woman lunged for Clio and I lunged for her. A shriek erupted. The frail cot scraped over the floor as I ensnared my talons around her delicate neck. A percussive sound rang in my ear. She clawed at my face like a wildling. I grimaced and grunted. The cot gave way beneath the kerfuffle. Then, we were an awkward tangle of limbs and bedsheets that reeked of BO and pubic hair.

Next thing I knew, fists were pounding into my jaw.

"Get off me!"

"Calm down, woman!" My words contorted with the incoming slam. *Sting.* She had a punch. I was on top of her and managed to grab her flailing wrists. I glared down at a twisted vision of lips and fangs. "I'm going to get up now and you are going to stop doing what you're doing, okay?"

Spidery veins splintered her brow. She clamped her mouth shut and nodded. That was when the door sprang open. Blade's voice was a cannon.

"What the hell is happening in here? We're attempting to sleep!"

Terrific. I had hoped to keep this little fiasco under wraps until dusk.

I climbed off the woman. She ignored the hand I offered to help her to her feet and fast adopted an indignant pose with hands on hips. I looked at Blade.

"We have a newborn clan member who needs to feed. Go and fetch one of the hawker males."

He gave a drawn-out whistle and looked beyond me to the woman.

"What's your name, sweetness?"

She gave a flick of her hair and lifted her chin.

"Leandra, and I'm not your sweetness."

11

THE FRENCH DEMILUNE WITCH

The air thinned as we ascended the ranges far west of Norbury city. Night sounds were few. My senses came alive despite the rough and uneven terrain. Branches slapped in my face as I led our group through twisted shrubs and thorny nettles.

Clio was adamant that we veer off deeper into the wilderness. I hoped she knew where we were going because I had no clue now.

Irritation was a tic in the back of my throat. I tried not to think about the wasted nights spent in that damned shack. Four to be exact. Turning Leandra kindred had slowed down our progress due to the time required for her to replenish her new energy. Now, we were tight on time, considering it was full-moon-glory the following night.

Fricken wolves and prophecies. They were the reason the world went to shit and so many lives destroyed. The reason I'd lost Scarla.

I groaned inwardly as Leandra's querulous voice rebounded from some place behind me. The regeneration process had no bearing on her temperament. If she was sassy before the transformation, she was now a pistol with a mouth.

"Argh! How much further?"

I didn't stop. She had fast acquired an entourage willing enough to cater to her every whim and she milked it for all its worth.

Hugo's deep drone replied. "Here Leandra, let me help you."

"Get your filthy hands off me, brute or I'll drain you of every last drop next time I feed."

He laughed. "Sounds promising."

A sharp inhale was followed by a slap. "You are a deplorable human. I'm sure Lord Marius will be interested to know how you disrespect female kindred members."

"I ... I'm sorry, Leandra. Forgive me."

Blade and Athan cracked up. I grinned.

"Yeah, cut him some slack, Leandra. He's just love-drunk on ya, is all!"

"He's like a Bryan Adams' number; he knows not what he does."

They broke out into an off-key version of *Please Forgive Me*. It sounded dreadful. Leandra huffed. Clio laughed. Hugo cackled. I smirked and imagined her snotty features twisting with her next words.

"Eh! How boring ... I hated Bryan Adams."

Athan guffawed.

"I heard tell he turned Death Metal since the apocalypse, jamming it up with Slayer these days."

More laughter ensued but I tuned out and picked up my pace, pushing through the dense undergrowth while Clio struggled to keep up beside me. Slivers of moonlight streamed through the thick forest canopy. I glanced at her.

"You chose an interesting candidate for your prophecy protection scheme."

She gave a subdued laugh. "I didn't choose her, you did."

"God help me."

"Ha. You mean God help all of us. She's a force to be reckoned with, but it's not her personality I'm interested in."

"Give it time."

I rubbed my temples. My thoughts strained.

According to Clio there was a little under an hour left between us and the wolf den. Why she needed Leandra's newborn vampire blood was a mystery.

I had to keep focused on the endgame – kill the baby and her mother. Return to Avila.

Simple. Well, it sounded simple enough in theory. I could only hope it played out the same way. *Lygarou. Who could've predicted the existence of such creatures?*

The fact that top federal agencies had not only known of the Lygarou but proceeded to abolish most of humanity through their defective ambitions to possess biological warfare, pissed me off no end.

I had spent hours in their underground city laboratory studying blood, blood-forming organs and blood diseases under an entirely false pretense. I felt like a fool.

Governments have a way of doing that. Can't say I looked forward to the backroom jungle awaiting our new bureaucracy. I repressed a shudder.

"Tell me about Evanora and Shane. Why did she create the Lygarou?"

Clio shook her head. "As far as I know, Evanora was a French Demilune witch who lived an isolated life in the mountains some time ago."

"How long some time ago?"

She shrugged. "About a hundred years or so.

Folklore says that the mountain wolves were drawn to her." She gave a half laugh. "A bit like the movie *Dances with Wolves*, only she was powerful enough to conjure a spell to bring the wolves into human form – with a sidekick that they would shift back into their former skins every full moon so that she was able to enjoy them as both animal and human. She called them Lygarou."

"*Dances with Wolves* in the literal sense."

She tittered lightly. Freckles like flecked gold. "Yes. Evanora and the Lygarou lived peacefully in the mountains for decades with no interference from the outside world."

"So, what happened?"

She pushed an overhanging branch aside to climb over a mound of earth. Her breath shortened, and she moved ahead of me on the path before answering.

"Shane is what happened. He was the first to be spawned – the alpha wolf. He grew bored of their isolated life and defied Evanora's sacred commandments." She stopped suddenly and looked at me, her voice grave. "The Lygarou were never supposed to be revealed to the world. They are a sacramental Demilune species with extraordinary gifts."

"Yeah, gifts that mutilate and kill."

"It was never supposed to be that way. The

reawakened are not of the sacred breed. They are Lystalkers."

Lystalkers. Lygarou. I didn't much care for labels when my daughter could be shredded. I didn't say as much though.

"Why are they different from the original breed?"

"Intent. When Shane deserted Evanora, she was beside herself with grief and fear. But she knew his decision to leave would inevitably expose her beloved Lygarou. Their utopian existence was gone. Everything was at risk – their lives and livelihood; their great honor, beliefs and tranquil code by which they lived. Even more so, Evanora was well aware of man's insatiable thirst for power. She couldn't have her wolves become subject to the scientific arena ..." Her voice trailed. "We all know how that goes."

"What did she do?"

"She did what any witch in her position would do; she conjured a dormant spell to suppress the species. Apparently, they sleep in peace within hidden caves some place deep in Sweetwater Valley."

I frowned. "Never heard of the place."

"Why would you? You're no witch."

"Good point." My thoughts were haywire. I didn't know which question I wanted answered next. I chose the obvious. "Why didn't her dormant spell work on Shane?"

Her fingers clutched at her jacket hem. She pulled the thin fabric tight around her. Her voice sounded somber.

"I think it was because he was the first to transform and mature into his werewolf abilities. His defiance was more than just an act of desertion; it caused a shift. Something to do with the time-belt; major alter fate-of-the-world stuff that eventuated into the V-virus." She shook her head. "He couldn't resurrect the original Lygarou without witchcraft, but he knew he could awaken an adapted breed by spawning a child."

Hmm ... the revelations were pouring forth and the cords in my neck vibrated. I looked ahead. My vision was exceptional now, particularly since my diet had been re-established into something sustainable.

I caught sight of movement among the thick brush bordering the trail. I halted and grabbed for Clio's hand just as the sound of Leandra's shrill voice blasted along the track.

For a split second, I froze, and everything happened at once. I spun around as a deep growl reverberated. Hugo screamed. Blade yelled blue murder.

I went to move but Leandra's pale, stricken features stole my vision as she sprinted toward me. She gripped my arm. Blade and Athan hissed, and Clio shrieked. Then, Leandra's hysterical voice stung my ears.

"W ... wolves!"

Fire ignited my veins. Thoughts evaporated. I flung my words over my shoulder as I pushed her aside and ran toward Hugo, Blade and Athan.

"Stay with Clio!"

12

PURE WILD

The winding trail blazed beneath my feet as I launched forward. I felt nothing but the mountain air whizzing across my skin. A hiss and a holler rose in the night. Rumbles and snarls erupted. The distinct sound of tearing flesh pricked my ears as I halted near Blade and Athan.

Incandescence. They were startling amber and pale blue, and they peered fiercely above exposed gums, thick canines and silver-tipped fur. I scanned the scene in a beat. Three wolves tore into Hugo. His massive figure writhed on the ground, and his wails were muffled.

Shit. My nerves were like razor wire. Three wolves stood between us and Hugo. Their legs were stiff; black hair bristled. Jaws dripped and teeth milled. One of them began to stalk back and forth. My nostrils scorched. *Wet dog.* It was blood and innards, and the musty odor of old rain that hung heavy in the air.

There was no time to dwell. I arched my shoulders and let out an insistent hiss. Supernatural adrenaline coursed through my veins. My vision flared. I surged forward, my talons shredding the air ahead of me. A roar ruptured in my throat. Athan and Blade moved like dynamite. The wolves hunched low, ears flattened. The stalking beast and I leapt at the same time. My bones crunched against solid matted hair and a wet snout as we collided in midair.

We plunged to the ground with a thud. His legs kicked in fury and his jaws enveloped my arm, his teeth sinking deep into flesh and veins. I barely felt it. I was hyped up. Thunderous growls detonated the air as I thrust my fist into his face and he shook his head, tearing at my arm.

Fuck. He wasn't letting go. Bats screeched with riotous shrills. My flesh stung. The others were going at it like monster alley on steroids. Dirt billowed. I let out a hiss and went for his eyes, plunging my talons into his sockets. I drove my talons deeper into his skull. The wolf yelped and instantly recoiled. Quilled paws slid across gravel. His eyes avoided mine as he gave a bark and a whimper and backed away. He raised his head and let out a long howl.

My stomach was a storm. Icy blue eyes flickered when he looked back at me. I hissed again and advanced toward him. I was ready for round two when the pack stopped suddenly and began to withdraw. Hugo groaned behind them as they retreated in seconds.

Blade's breath was heavy beside me. "Holy mother of all things wild, what the fuck was that?"

I glanced at him and Athan. Their features were spidery lines of blue on white. Blood stained Athan's skull and hands. Blade's golden stare was a crimson moon.

I shrugged. "Wolves."

"Yeah, no shit." Athan said. "Wolves on what? Animals don't usually behave like that."

I gave him a frown. "And since when do humans behave like vampires, hmm?"

He said nothing as Leandra and Clio emerged from the trees unharmed. Relief was fleeting. If this was the welcoming party, I shuddered to think what was waiting for us at the wolf-mother's den.

Clio faced me. "You okay?"

Stupid question. I was a vampire. I healed fast. I nodded and she promptly went to Hugo. The dirt trail beneath him was clotted with blood. His dreadlocks were soaked through and his clothes were shredded to reveal torn flesh and many gaping holes. I didn't hold out much hope for him considering his state.

Clio crouched over Hugo and glanced at me. "He's still alive!"

"Yes." I moved closer to peer at him. His face was a mash-up of meaty flesh and blood soup. I shook my head. "I don't think he will be for much longer."

He gurgled and squirmed. It was arduous.

"We best be getting on with it," Blade said. "The sun will be up before long."

He was right. It was only a matter of hours until dawn and we still had to face the wolves if we were to secure lodgings for the day. Of course, we had no choice but to set our sights on the wolf den as coverage.

Clio stood up and scowled. "We can't just leave him like this! It's seriously undignified!"

She might be right. I may have been indifferent toward him, but he did provide mouthfuls of blood here and there to keep us sustained. I studied him. Big mammoth human who had chosen to be a Shadow Guardian in our new world. *Schmuck.*

I was about to respond to Clio when Leandra pushed past me and halted in front of him. Her hands gripped her waist and her breasts pushed forward as she peered at him. She gave an exaggerated flick of her long hair before narrowing her eyes at me. "May I?"

Surprise rippled through me, but I remained silent and nodded. She mirrored my move before dropping to her knees before him. Her scarlet skirt fanned out like a blossom dream as she tenderly took his chin between her palms and murmured in his ear.

"I'm sending a dove to heaven." She pressed her lips to his forehead and spoke against his skin. "I forgive you, dummy."

He groaned and blinked as he reached to stroke her cheek. She smiled down at him and everything began to feel hollow. *Heart.* It banged in my chest. My breath stalled as she stretched his neck to the side and sunk her fangs into his throat. He didn't make a sound. His chest deflated and his body slumped further into the dirt. I was completely floored.

13

RUMBLE IN THE WOODS

Illusion. Horror. Savagery.

Treetops swayed with the slight breeze and silver clouds doused the moon. The forest hummed. We stood amid the dewy trunks that fringed the clearing and we peered at the wolf den. I inhaled. Wildflowers and rotting wood lingered along with the scent of hostility.

"Well now, I can't say that my visions of the wolf den resembled anything remotely like that." Blade rubbed his chin and glanced at Clio. "You sure this is the right place? Maybe you need to check your witch GPS again."

He had a point. The wolf den turned out to be an enormous log cabin with lofty peaked rooftops, sprawling verandas and floor-to-ceiling windows that glowed from within. It was a far cry from a den, whatever that looked like.

Athan laughed.

Clio scowled. "Dick."

Blade stepped up to her. "You negate me with your name calling?" He reached to stroke a lock of her hair. "Let's see how that works out for you in the immediate future."

She gave him a sharp elbow. "Is that a threat, Barnacle?"

He backed away, his face contorted with the shadows.

"Just pointing out the obvious. We're all equipped to handle the Lystalkers. I don't see no fangs on your honeypot gums."

She was about to retort when I cut in. "Shut up!" I flicked my chin toward the den. "We've got the right place."

Illusion.

Sometimes reality felt surreal. This was one of those moments. The log cabin door flung open to reveal a brawny hooded figure. He paused at the threshold. His eyes were shadowed above a protruding chin spread with dark stubble. His broad shoulders were like a giant as he stepped from the cabin to stand at the top of the stairs.

He looked straight at me as a pack of wolves emerged from around the back of the cabin along with ten other men who spilled onto the veranda. They clutched an array of weapons – stakes and swords, and a couple of chains. They stunk offensively and stood with pinched expressions and glassy stares as one wolf raised his head to give a long howl.

A chill went through me. *Was this a waking dream?* My hammering heart suggested otherwise. That and Leandra's sudden needled grip on my arm.

"There is only five of us, Jett!"

"I'm aware." I pried her fingers from my arm. "You're about to get a fast lesson in supernatural combat. Watch for stakes and avoid wolf jaws. Be who you were reborn to be and stay close to me." I glanced at Blade and Athan whose eyes were like hot steel. "Keep an eye on the witch."

They grunted a reply while Clio flicked out a switchblade. She held it steady and nodded. I braced myself before we moved from the trees and into the clearing. Adrenaline rushed. My veins felt twitchy, and the wolfmen were on the move.

They descended the stairs and strode toward us. The Lystalker front line sneered, exposing grotty teeth. They were clad in dirty denim and checkered shirts. I could only be grateful they were still in human form but their menacing grins were accompanied by a disturbing chorus of snarls emanating from their four-legged friends slinking alongside them.

Horror.

I was a creature of death who longed to kill. My fingers prickled. Aggression pulsed. The earth felt spongy and the air hung dense as we stopped mid-way and faced them. Bestial blood called my name as the big fellow shrugged his hood from his head and looked at me. Cold eyes dilated.

"I figured there would be more of you."

"We don't need more."

His bulbous nostrils flared with his grin. "Now that's a bold statement if I ever heard one."

I laughed. "Want to hear another one?"

Gray eyes flickered. His grin dissolved as I moved with the swiftness of the wind. Roars and growls crackled in my ears. My hands found his throat in a searing flash. He resisted. His strength was a revelation, but I was a demon. A fiend searching for blood. My talons etched deep as my fangs pierced the flesh as I bit down hard.

He bellowed. It was hellish. Twisted shrieks became the night as fists like cannons punched me in the side of the head. The impact jarred me. Thwacks and grunts, and butchered flesh. I grimaced and gripped him harder.

Bones crunched against my fangs. One brutal shove and I was reeling backward. A chunk of raw wolfman meat filled my mouth.

Salt and metal.

I regained my footing and crouched. I spat out his flesh, scanning the riot. *Massacre.* It smelled like home. I caught the scene all at once: Wolves prowled and ravaged. Vampires were like light. Blade danced with iron jaws snapping at his ankles as he thrashed his claws along a wolfman's face and hissed. Chains whizzed. Athan growled like an inferno and tore off a head. Swords clanked to the ground. Leandra was spectral – grace and evil. Clio was nowhere in sight.

"Jett!"

Leandra gestured quickly. The big guy howled and ran for me. He had a stake. I sprung to my feet and charged for him, dodging the sharp end of the stave and plunging my fist through his chest. Bone on bone. His ribcage shattered. *Warmth.* He froze. His stubble jaw slackened as my palm encircled his heart.

Savagery.

I felt nothing as I leaned to speak into his ear. "Bold statement is bold heart."

He gasped as I clenched the throbbing organ and yanked it from him. I spun around, barely hearing his body thud to the ground as a wolf lunged at me. *Boom.* It was solid. I hit the ground to gaping jaws, hot breath and a soggy nose.

I shoved him hard. My flesh ripped. I hooked an arm around his thick neck and slammed my fist into his head. An ensemble of high pitched screeches peeled across the night sky. I glanced up. *Bats.* They were everywhere. A vision of black wings as they swarmed and swooped.

Disorientation. It was momentary. Pitch wings, red eyes and sharp beaks were our allies. They barraged the wolves in an incessant onslaught. The mammoth beast on top of me grizzled as bats tore at his ears and eyes. He yelped and I rolled from beneath him.

A fast breath and thumping hooves. *What the hell?* I turned toward the forest to catch sight of a herd of deer. They appeared from the brush like a doe-eyed vision and were heading straight for us. That was when the bats receded to a low hover and wolf ears pricked. Alert eyes were reduced to slivers; jaws salivated, and canine hair bristled before gigantic paws were set into motion.

My mind whirled as bleats and squeals rose like a city circus. Dust clouded. Jaws clipped furiously. The herd bolted from the clearing and made for the forest as the wolves gave chase beneath a flock of wild bats.

I frowned, and it was as heavy as the cloak of silence that followed. My back panged as I looked around. Leandra, Blade and Athan stood like blood-soaked mullets staring into the woods. Bodies and carnage littered the clearing. It was a mess. The wolfmen were goners. *Dead.* A moment felt like forever.

"Where's Clio?"

"I'm here!"

She stood at the top of the log cabin stairs and waved at me. Respite was my next breath until I spotted the woman behind her crossing the cabin threshold. Skintight black leather appeared sprayed to her body and contrasted against the tumble of golden hair that fell over one shoulder as she sidled up beside Clio. Her thick lashes blinked over large amber eyes as they settled on me. My heart lurched.

Scarla?

Everything was numb after that.

14

WHEN THE PAST COMES CALLING

"Jett?" Leandra's touch startled me. My boots seeped into the earth. "Are you okay?"

Did my eyes betray me? I couldn't stop looking at her. My bottom lip slackened but I managed to nod. "Let's get inside."

I walked like a ghost. My mind was a fog. Perhaps the blows to my head had more impact than I thought. The wolfman *did* pack a meaty punch.

I saw her throat split. I saw her die.

My breath splintered when she turned away and vanished inside the cabin, and I barely heard Athan and Blade's discussion as we took the steps up to the veranda. Clio's dark stare held mine. Her features were unreadable.

"What was with the Zootopia scene?" Athan said.

"Mystery. Maybe the witch is in the know." Blade came to an abrupt halt in front of Clio. He gazed at her through the bloodied flaxen locks shadowing his brow. "It was you, wasn't it?"

"Some simple spells stuck from the time spent with my grandmother."

He gave a low whistle before grinning.

"Respect!" He gestured toward the cabin. "I need to get cleaned up before my slumber. Do they have running water in there or what?"

Her nose scrunched. "How should I know?"

He grunted a reply before moving past her, and Athan and Leandra followed him into the house. A strange feeling took hold as I watched them. Half of me wanted to get to the woman inside as fast as possible. The half couldn't move. It was Clio's voice that set me in motion.

"Come on. The sun is almost up, you need to get inside."

She was right. I'd hardly noticed the perpetual murky hues on the horizon. My chest felt tight as I followed her inside, and I halted as soon as I crossed the threshold, barely hearing the door slam shut behind me as Clio set about shutting off the house to the impending sunlight. The sounds of yanking curtains, banging doors and clanking shutters were lost on me as I looked around.

Evergreen and Peach.

It was those soft woody scents of cedar that encapsulated my senses. It was rather nice, and so was the lofty timber ceiling that was suspended over oil-stained floorboards and sandstone walls. If you were inclined to notice it like that. I couldn't go there. But as my gaze swept over the thick pile rugs that sprawled beneath oversized sofas and polished furniture, I did notice the set of stone stairs that created a focal point that spiraled toward the upper levels.

My nostrils twitched. The place had a somewhat calm vibe, but that was the last thing I felt when my vision settled on the woman who sat in the far corner nursing her child. My nerves were as sharp as the look in her whiskey colored eyes as she held her swaddled baby and scowled. A slice of heaven moved through me. *I knew those eyes.* My gaze latched onto hers and I was transported to another place. *Scarla.* She was just like her – the clean shape of her cheekbones beneath porcelain skin; the delicate etches of her lips and the way her hair wisped around her jawline. Even the slight crease on her brow mirrored the woman I had loved.

Bella donna.

The resemblance was uncanny. Nothing was

making sense, but I knew I had to get my shit together. We were on the home stretch. We'd faced the wolfman pack and their hounds protecting her, secured the wolf den and now she was within arm's reach. All I needed to do was to kill her and the kid and this entire Lystalker fiasco would be behind us. Peace would be restored to the clan and my daughter would be safe.

Pièce de résistance. She was mine.

I ignored the others buzzing around the place as they called out to each other from unseen parts of the house. They were scouting every nook and cranny before our slumber. We all knew the threat was far from over and we were at our most vulnerable through the day. Luckily, we had a witch on our side who could keep watch.

Grace eluded me as I moved ahead. The woman reacted instantly by shrinking back into her chair. She clutched the baby tighter and her paling lips quavered.

"Who ... who are you? What do you want from us?"

I gasped and paused. *Silver bells.* The timbre of voice sounded just like Scarla's. I shook my head and said her name without thinking.

"Scarla?"

"Huh?" Her mouth fell apart and she sprung to her feet. The baby gurgled as she rushed closer to me. I could smell the powdery scent of the newborn baby and the sweet sweat glistening on her brow. *Blossoms.*

She sneered in my face. "You're a vampire; how do you know my mother?"

Every so often, life presents us with information that blows our minds. I was nullified. Words felt distant. Her jaw squared and eyes like transpicuous lanterns flashed as she scrutinized me. Tingles shimmied up my spine and that was when I knew it to be true. The wolf-mother was Scarla's daughter. A daughter I never knew existed.

"You're Scarla's daughter?" I could barely keep my voice steady. "Scarla Mage?"

"Yes. Who are you?"

"Jett."

"Jett?" Her eyes widened. "You're Jett?"

This was getting too much. Ludicrous even. She had obviously heard about me. I was about to answer when the baby cooed and squirmed in her arms. My gaze went to the little bundle to catch sight of tiny fists jarring through the air. All at once, I felt pitted as I watched tiny knuckles turn white. Her mother began rocking back and forth as she watched me. My throat rumbled.

"You're the wolf-mother." It wasn't a question. Hardly even a coherent thought. She responded regardless.

"My name is Sienna and this is Shana, Scarla's granddaughter."

"She carries the Blood Legend code in her genes – half wolf, half human."

Her eyes darkened to inkwells.

"Half human with the rare blood. That's why her birth is so critical for the future. You have to help me protect her."

Whaat? Rare blood? Scarla's bloodline carried the AB positive blood that had eventuated in her death?

I struggled for clarity as a heaviness weighed in my limbs. I couldn't even summon a response. Her next question nailed my tongue to the roof of my mouth.

"Is my mother with you? Is she safe?"

My stomach dropped. She didn't know Scarla was dead. I ground my teeth and met her stare. I didn't need to say the words out loud. My expression revealed all she needed to know. Her face twisted and went gaunt as realization dawned, and the look in her eyes tore at my soul.

"I'm sorry ..." My voice was unfamiliar. This scene was unfamiliar. Her raw pain reminded me of my lost humanity. A glimmer in the eye. *Light.* I wanted to touch her; to offer comfort of some sort. It was at that moment Clio decided to make an entrance, walking into the room with her energy all keyed-up.

"Okay, I've battened up the house as much as I can. There are showers and soap upstairs. You should consider using both before your slumber." She halted abruptly but I didn't look at her. I was too busy watching Sienna's heart shatter before my eyes. Guilt was a creeping shadow, as was Clio as she drew closer.

"What's going on?"

My eyes darted. "She ..." I gestured toward Sienna. "I know her."

"Huh?" Clio balked before her hair became a scorching vision as she shook her head. I briefly wondered if her eyes would pop from their sockets. "Umm ... well, isn't this a surprise?" Hands clasped hips; a cool stare sized up the situation. "You realize this doesn't change anything, Jett. The kid needs to die to stop the Lystalkers."

Sienna shrieked. She began to edge backward. "What? You came here to kill us? My baby? No way!"

I held up my palms and moved toward her, stopping when her wild eyes pinned my boots to the floor. The baby began to cry as she spun around and made a dash for a door at the far end of the room. I called out to her, but my voice was lost against her high-pitched scream as Blade suddenly burst through the door.

His face was contorted with a vicious hiss. She

gripped the baby and stepped back as his face split into a sly grin.

"Going somewhere, my sweetness?"

Her throat swelled slightly before she whirled around, almost tripping over a rug as she bolted toward the center of the room. Athan and Leandra appeared from another doorway. Her boots twisted on the floor and the baby wailed in her arms as her eyes skimmed between us. She shook her head.

"Please ... don't hurt my baby."

Scarla.

She blinded me. Everything felt knotted and my mouth ran dry as Blade's voice grated over the bawling baby. Lemon eyes gleamed my way.

"It's time for you to complete your retribution, Jett." He gestured toward Sienna. "And make it quick; we could all use an early slumber."

Sienna's eyes were dewy when they met mine. Agony gripped me from the inside out. I had no choice but to kill the daughter and granddaughter of the woman I had loved more than anything. The woman I couldn't keep safe from this ugly world. The lives of the surviving humans and the clan depended on their deaths. So did the life of my own daughter. I couldn't even feel the tips of my fingers. I was obliterated.

15

THE SILENCE

*S*ilence.

It felt like violence. The moments preceding death were anointed with annihilation. It chilled me to the bone. Clio's breath was audible. She stood somewhere behind me. Shana's cries muffled beneath my thumping heart as I lowered my chin to gage the situation with my senses.

Blade, Athan and Leandra advanced toward Sienna who began to sob and shake her head. *Heat.* I could feel her throbbing pulse as they closed in around her. Blade cackled. His footsteps were like synaptic impulses in my brain.

"There, there, my sweetness. It will be over in a jiffy."

Sienna's shrill deafened. I closed my eyes. Vampire

fever burned my nostrils. Headiness rimmed like vitality. Athan's voice was an explosive staccato.

"Wake up, slayer! Plenty of time to slumber after you complete the kill."

His chunky tongue ran across his bottom lip as I looked at him. He grinned and motioned toward Sienna.

"You gotta do it now, before the Lystalkers get a chance to re-skin tonight."

I knew that he was right. If the half-breed wasn't destroyed, the Lystalkers would attack the city tonight with the full moon. Vampires and humans alike would perish, and Marius would know of my failure long before our return to the city. He would kill Avila and Sun.

I gave a heavy sigh and looked at Sienna. She stood stiff as she clutched Shana near a coffee table. Her lips were like jelly and her eyes stole my breath as she silently pleaded with me. *Torment.* It was Scarla all over again and the scene felt the same. The day the hawkers came to slice her throat and dump her body in the dust near my feet. The day I had lost a part of my soul.

Leandra's sudden outcry broke my reverie.

"Hurry up, Jett! We haven't got all day; I want to go clean up."

It was time. I inhaled sharply and strode toward them. All eyes were glued on me as I stopped short of

Sienna. She gazed up at me through the tears that now splashed against her cheeks. I shook my head.

"I'm sorry."

Her eyes widened and terror claimed her features. Blade laughed. Athan grunted. *Exhale.* My senses were acute. I clenched my fists. Adrenaline pumped as I whirled around and smashed my knuckles through Blade's chest. Shock struck his face as Leandra shrilled and Athan roared behind me.

Athan barged into me. Meaty arms ensnared my chest. I braced myself and snarled. I grabbed the back of Blade's skull. Broken ribs splintered as I followed the thrust of the motion and palmed his heart.

Life.

His was literally in the palm of my hands. Athan growled and yanked me hard. This time, I didn't resist. My boots stumbled backward with the weight of him behind me. Blade's eyes bulged like neon lights as his heart slipped from his body as I fell against Athan.

He slumped to the floor, but I didn't hear the thud. Athan's inky eyes raged as I turned to catch him lunging for me.

"Motherfucker!"

His talons ripped through the air and slashed across my cheeks. I sprung back and pegged Blade's heart at him, following with a hiss and a round of blows to his head. He didn't even budge with the impact. His growl was like the grim reaper as he caught one of my flailing fists.

Silence.

Pain erupted in my hand beneath his vise-like grip and my bones shattered as he squeezed with brutal force. I grunted. It sounded contorted as we staggered around before I flung my other hand at his face, going for his eyes. My razor talons scratched at cold flesh and blood rushed beneath my nails. He dodged a jab to the eye. His putrid breath blew over my face and his other fist was solid muscle as he pounded it into my temple.

Dizziness threatened. Black spots stained my vision. Infant wails and screams cut through my head as my legs gave way. I fell hard. Athan's weight was debilitating as he clambered on top of my back. He had me pinned to the floor. He clobbered his fists into my spine and let out a barrage of profanities.

"You double-crossing, wolf-loving piece of shit!"

A hiss sounded nefarious. My ears began ringing. My jaw felt like a boxing match against the hard floor as my whirling vision found the leg of a coffee table. Timber. My thoughts tunneled as he paused in his barrage and leaned over me.

"You killed my friend and broke kindred law. I'm going to take your heart before I murder the mongrels.

And then I'm going to tear your daughter apart with my big vampire cock before I slaughter her."

I tensed. Blood oozed like sticky paint.

"Like hell you will."

Violent silence.

It was a fleeting second. He went to move and as his weight shifted, I reached for the coffee table leg and wrenched it as hard as I could. The timber paling cracked as I tore it from the tabletop and a series of clunks followed. I gripped the wooden stave and roared, twisting my body around at the same time that he went to plunge his fist through the flesh of my back.

Strike. The stave found its target. His lips sagged and his catapulting fist went off course as I shoved the paling through his chest and into his heart. Time stalled. Burly fingers fumbled at the stake as I drove it in harder. He wheezed and gasped for air. His chest sucked against his ribs like a deflating balloon as scarlet saliva pooled over his bottom lip and his face went ashen. Then, he dropped like a sack of potatoes and I rolled away from him.

Silence.

No longer did it feel like violence.

LITTLE SECRETS

"What the hell did you do?" Leandra struck her heels into the floor and peered down at me. Blue veins lumped across her brow. "You killed them, Jett!"

My eyes fixed on the timber fan blades that suspended from the pitched ceiling. I felt depleted and my back hurt. "I do know that, Leandra."

She huffed and puffed like a dragon and flailed her arms wide as she hissed down at me. "What were you thinking? Now, we're all dead. If Marius doesn't get us first then the Lystalkers will, thanks to you!"

I knew she was not too far off the mark; my thought process wasn't even clear to me. *What was I thinking?* Only hours before I was hankering to kill the wolf family and get on with my new kindred life. Now, I had just done the one thing that I had vowed to avoid – I'd jeopardized the life of my daughter. *Have I lost my mind?* All I knew was that I couldn't allow Sienna and Shana to die today. Scarla had been too precious and too important to me. Even in death, I wasn't going to fail her again.

Unfortunately, that choice came with dire consequences that I now had to face, and I had no plan for the immediate future. I grimaced and stood. My legs felt like pudding as I regarded Blade and Athan. They slumped on the floor like shriveled gray carcasses smeared with blood. It was too bad. A part of me was just beginning to warm up to them. Somewhat.

"What are we going to do, Jett?" Leandra gripped her hips. Dried blood and grime shadowed the creases on her scrunched nose. "You sired me into this dumb-ass mess. How are you going to get me out of it?" She gestured toward Sienna who now sat nursing the child and silently staring at us. "We can still kill the half-breed and save ourselves."

Sienna was all volcano. "Like fuck you will, barnacle-bitch."

Leandra's eyes narrowed. "That's tough talk for a rabies-bitten slag without her dogs."

Sienna stood up. "Oh, they will come. Do you really think Shane would leave his child for too long?" Copper eyes boiled. "He's recruiting more of us for tonight's full lunar when *you* get to become vampire stew."

"All the more reason to dice the kid." Leandra hissed at me. "Did you hear her? We have to do something!"

God help me.

"Shut up, Leandra. Go take your shower so I can think."

I rubbed my temple. My hand felt like a bag of grainy sand; the one that Athan had so lovingly crushed. I wasn't regenerating as fast as usual. Blood and sleep deprivation will do that to a vampire. Throw in a few violent brawls and I was naked. My veins felt like withered spaghetti. I hadn't had a decent feed since we shared the last hawker male a few days ago. If you could call that decent.

Leandra's mouth formed a huge "O" before clamping shut. I could almost see the gears turning in her head. *Ding ding.* Something appealed. She gave an indignant nod. "Very well, but I hope your *thinking* wields more desirable results than our current predicament."

I ignored her glare. "Go."

She gave a dramatic flick of her head and about-faced before stalking from the room. I exhaled and immediately collapsed onto a sofa, momentarily relishing the soft folds against my back and searching out

Clio with my eyes. I found her standing in a shadowy corner by the cabin entrance. Her fingers knotted and she chewed on her bottom lip.

"You're awfully quiet," I said. "Nothing to say about the sudden turn of events?"

She moved from the corner and her eyes appeared somber as she walked closer. I kept quiet and watched as she pushed back unruly hair and stopped in front of me. I swallowed a knowing sigh. She had been adamant that the baby's death was the only way to protect what was left of humanity against the Lystalkers. I'd be lying if I didn't say that I wasn't expecting another tongue-lashing. I was ready for it.

She caught me off guard when she slid to her knees and reached for my hands. A moment of respite found me as skin like a sunny day wrapped around the chill of mine.

"You're weak," she said.

"I've had better days."

She pulled her hands from mine and my insides instantly protested. I barely noticed that she had rolled up her jacket sleeve until she thrust her wrist into my face. "Drink."

I gaped at her and briefly considered a refusal, but then the sweet rhythm of her pulse caught my ear in a lullaby and my willpower was none to zero. Hunger brimmed in my eyes as they met hers. She gave a nod and I cupped her wrist between my palms and paused. *Ba boom. Ba boom.* The sound of her heart became a rapid beat. I dropped my eyes to the smooth flesh of wrist before my own heart surged and I lowered my lips to find the tangy bliss of her blood.

Delectation.

It raptured in my veins like rich merlot, but I was careful not to take too much from her – only what I needed to nourish my body before slumber. Her quickening breath and frantic pulse were my cue to withdraw from her flesh. *Sour cherry and spice.* It clung to my lips as she immediately wrapped her arm in a cloth as I leaned back into the sofa and allowed the fresh blood to fuse within me. After a few moments, I began to feel normal enough to gather my thoughts.

Time to think my way out of this situation. I looked at Sienna. Her expression was passive, but her eyes flickered at me as Shana slept bundled in a bassinet by her feet. She gave a waning smile.

"Thank you."

I nodded in reply as Clio clasped my hands again.

"Feel a little better?"

"Yes." My voice sounded awkward. "Thank you, I never would've asked."

"I know." She grinned. "Look at you go, pure heart."

"Pure heart just committed murder against his own kind and disobeyed his kindred master." I flicked my chin toward the infant. "Nothing is alright, the kid still breathes."

"She does. The Blood Legend legacy will pass through the generations because of you – you've protected the prophecy."

Huh? Hold on a second.

"This pleases you? You wanted her dead; you said it was the only way to ensure the survival of humans."

A smile split her face. "I did say that, didn't I?" She leapt to her feet and her mouth offered a fast script as she began pacing. "It had to be this way, Jett. The choice had to be yours despite the pressure from others and the outside world – you did this – it was the only way a cloaking spell of this magnitude could work."

"Cloaking spell? What are you talking about?"

She stopped abruptly and looked at me.

"Shana can't die, Jett. If she dies, the Blood Legend gene dies with her, leaving us facing a bleak future with no hope." Her eyes gleamed. "Her blood is just the beginning. She must procreate to allow the genes time to evolve through the generations. It will be her granddaughter who will arrive during the transition era to ignite the second apocalypse."

My mind was a ticking timebomb. "But what about

the Lystalkers? They're still going to be around to wipe everyone out long before that. They're too primitive, not of the original bloodline. You said so yourself."

"The Lystalkers won't be a threat when the cloaking spell is created. It will render them dormant."

A sprig of hope shimmied through me.

"Then, Marius won't know the difference between the kid being alive or dead." I was almost afraid to believe it. "Avila will be safe."

"And so will the humans – at least, the ones you lot don't kill. The ones who are becoming the first generation of Leavings." She gestured toward Sienna. "But I have to get them to Sweetwater Valley before the full moon tonight; and somehow, I will have to find Alvin."

"Alvin?"

"Yeah, he's the only one that can do something like this. All I need is Leandra to bite the kid so that her newborn kindred blood merges with Shana's – this acts as a blood shield and bonds the two bloodlines." She frowned and began pacing again. "I'll also need some kind of matching lockets to act as dual components to hold each supernatural element and guard the cloaking spell; Alvin can do the rest. He lives in the valley, I think."

"You think? Clio ..."

She cut in. "Remember what I said about faith?"

My eyes narrowed but I said nothing. She wasn't waiting for my reply anyway.

"Well, I'm asking you to have faith now. It's either that or things are going to get a whole lot worse come tonight." She paused to look at Sienna. "Only Alvin can make a spell of this magnitude happen. Will you come with me?"

A few moments felt like forever.

Sienna squared her jaw. "Marius has your daughter, Avila?"

"Yes. He will kill her when he discovers my betrayal."

Her eyes glazed. "My mother used to talk about Avila. She was very fond of her and said that we would've made great friends."

My heart hollowed at the mention of Scarla. But it was confusion that prevailed over my emotions.

"I don't doubt that for one minute." I shook my head. "Your mother told you about us? Why did she never tell me about you?"

She gave a rueful laugh. "She had no choice. Nobody could know about me. The risk was too great, what with Shane being kept prisoner for all those years in a government lab."

"Why could no one know of you?" Clio asked.

Sienna lifted her eyes to mine and for some reason, my breath almost stopped.

"Because not only do I carry the rare blood now sought by the kindred, but my father was a direct descendant of the Lygarou originals."

Clio's gasp hardly penetrated my astonishment.

STARGAZER

"*Stargazer, you call the shots and I take em.*"

She used to whisper to the stars and speak with angels. Of that, I was sure. My stargazing woman was too good for a world like this. She had to leave. Her soul was too pure. The vermin now infecting the world would have spoiled her from the inside out. Yet, I would selfishly give anything to have her back.

She out of mind and simply out of soul.

Stargazer: Mother Love Bone.

It played in my mind and dragged at my heart as I watched Scarla's daughter lay down her child to receive the bite of a newborn vampire. That song could have been written for Scarla – the best thing I'd ever seen. My eyes fell to the infant who lay on top of a small white blanket. Rosebud lips and dimpled cheeks. Golden hair and innocence. She would never know the woman I loved.

The moments felt as if shrouded with divinity and I knew they were among the last that I would spend with Scarla's family. Another piece of her would be ripped from my life as fast as it had appeared, but they would survive, and that, along with Avila, has become my priority. Scarla and the magnificent secrets flowing through her bloodlines were the key to the future. Even beyond her death, my woman was still a gift to the world. I felt privileged for the little time I had shared with her. Somehow, my love for Scarla had brought me to her daughter and reminded me of all that was lost to the kindred existence – our ability to feel emotions and love.

Sienna hesitated before stepping away from the baby. *Myrrh and Frankincense.* It was distinctive and floral, and it burned with the curling scent of incense as strong as the uncertainty filling her eyes.

"If you see Shane, tell him that I'm sorry. Tell him where I've gone."

"I will. You're doing the right thing."

She bit her lip and gave a fast nod. This wasn't easy for her. She was choosing to take her daughter and abandon her lover for the sake of preserving the survival of humans. These were the days when every choice made was accompanied with critical consequences. Her choice would see the end to Shane's quest in taking vengeance against those who had mistreated him – a vendetta that would cause more suffering for humanity.

Clio rested a hand on Sienna's shoulder. "It will be okay. Alvin will take good care of you and Shana."

Her dark gaze skimmed to me briefly before she went to the baby. She held a small bag of salt and two heart shaped pendants suspended on thin gold chains that Sienna had produced. She paused over Shana and smiled.

"Hey sweet little one, you're going to save a lot of people; you're going to do great things but you have to brave now, okay?"

Shana pushed a balled fist into her mouth. Her eyelids began to close. That was when Clio began to whisper in a dialect I couldn't decipher as she placed one pendant above Shana's head and the other at her feet. After that, she created a wide circle of salt around the infant before positioning five white candles on the circle at even intervals and lighting them. She stood up and reached into her pocket to produce a switchblade, flicking it open as she motioned for Leandra.

"Show me your wrists."

Oddly enough, Leandra was silent as she exposed the smooth flesh of her wrists to the sharp end of the blade. Clio sliced into her skin and blood rushed to the surface.

"You must enter the altar to bestow on her the Threefold Kiss. You will bite her lips that shall utter sacred names; her heart that shall form her strength, and her third eye that shall see all." Clio's voice deepened. "Your bite must break her skin only so that she may take your blood with her own. Do not feed on her, do you understand?"

Leandra nodded. Her expression was passive, but the slight tremble of her lips betrayed her nerves as she stepped into the sacred circle. Her feet anchored apart as she looked down at the sleeping baby. Her voice was barely audible.

"I'm sorry ... this is going to hurt just a little bit."

She bent to her knees and Clio began to chant words that sounded charming and foreign. Witch lingo. The pitch of her voice rose and fell in a lilting melody and created an unusual sensation through me. It felt profound, as if the unfolding ritual was a momentous event that would forever alter history. It was everything surreal.

Dancer, dancer. I'm all wrong.

Shana's cries rose above Leandra as she performed the Threefold Kiss; gently pressing her fangs into the soft folds of baby skin before allowing her blood to drip into the broken flesh. Sienna tensed beside me. I cringed and looked away to the fragrant haze that hovered over them. I gasped when I saw Scarla's figure dancing in the curling incense smoke.

Scarla?

Hands clasped sensual hips that swayed beneath a swirling white dress. Long lashes shadowed her cheeks while lustrous flaxen hair flowed down her back as she moved with grace. *Angel.* Lips like swollen cherries smiled as she whirled around before fixing her eyes on me. The sound of her voice was heaven in my soul.

"Dance with me."

"I'm an awful dancer."

"You're wrong."

My heart cracked wide open as her essence shrouded me. *My love.* Clio's chants became an intense backdrop as I arched my neck and lifted my arms and surrendered to her. I would have fallen to my knees and given her everything I had left. I would die all over again for her. Anything for her. I closed my eyes and my lips moved without a sound.

"I'll dance with your soul every day. Wait for me."

"Always."

The faint sound of her reply echoed through my mind as the Threefold Kiss ritual was completed. Scarla was gone and I felt heady. I blinked to see Leandra wipe her lips with the back of a hand as she stepped from the circle. Sienna immediately went to console her child and the energy in the room shifted into the stark reality we faced. It was Leandra's voice that hit me next.

"May I go upstairs to slumber now?"

"Yes, go. I'll see them off and join you shortly," I said.

She gripped her hips.

"Good. Let's hope all this hocus-pocus stuff keeps us alive long enough to replenish ourselves."

I forced a smile. "You better go get your head start then."

She didn't say anything else as she strutted from the room. I was relieved that she didn't stick around to bid the others farewell. While she had obviously taken a crucial role in what had just transpired, I sensed that she was about as trustworthy as a shady King Street pimp on ICE. To say I was concerned was an understatement.

Clio stuffed the heart pendants into her jacket pocket. She ran a hand through her unruly auburn hair as she came up beside me.

"We have to get going while we still have enough daylight."

"I know."

They were making the journey to Sweetwater Valley alone. I couldn't join them; my place was back in the city with my daughter. Besides, no one could know for sure if they would make it to the valley and find the elusive Alvin before tonight's full moon. I planned on leaving here as soon as I could to get to Avila. This was far from over yet.

Clio reached for my hand.

"Get some rest; you're going to need it."

I was indeed. My body ached. Sleep was a relentless tendril pushing behind my eyes. At least we didn't have humans to slow us down during the journey back to Norbury. Leandra and I could run like the wind.

"What about Leandra? She might speak of this. She's a risk."

"Not for long. Her blood is now infused with Shana's. As soon as Alvin completes the ritual that I just began, her memory of this will be cloaked along with the spell."

Relief didn't come. "If you find him, that is."

"You got to believe in something, Jett. It may as well be this."

"I don't have much choice."

She cupped a palm over my heart. "We always have a choice, pure heart."

I couldn't help but smile. "You're a rainbow, alright. Make sure you ride the colors to the end." I gestured toward Sienna who now stood near the cabin door with a rucksack and holding a bundled Shana. "Look after them."

"I will. Goodbye, Jett."

I stroked the side of her cheek with the back of my knuckles. Her skin was like warm milk.

"Maybe we'll meet again someday."

She grinned.

"If we don't, we always have the afterlife."

"Yeah."

My thoughts went to Scarla and the familiar ache dredged my heart.

Stargazer won't you kick with me (again).

18

FULL MOON RENDEZVOUS

*H*ands shook me violently from a deep sleep.

"Jett, wake up!" Leandra's voice was frantic. I struggled to get my bearings. "We overslept. They're here!"

Whaat?

She leapt to her feet and rushed to the window of the room where we had chosen to rest, and yanked back the thick curtains to reveal the night sky. I sat up and swung my legs from the bed, catching sight of the full moon shining from an inky canvas. My stomach curled as a long predatory growl sounded from the level below.

"Shane."

My nostrils flared with the distinct odor of a base human scent mixed with wolf. It was that strong, I could smell him even from beneath the gap of the closed bedroom door. My thoughts stormed like a whirlwind. The Lystalkers had transformed and were on the prowl. Obviously, Clio hadn't found the great sorcerer Alvin in time to stop the change.

Avila.

I had to get to her. My chest constricted as I stood up and Leandra gasped. Her eyes flashed neon red through the dark.

"We have to leave – now!"

I wasn't going to argue that point. "The window."

It was our only option. A fierce snarl chilled my bones. The sound of heavy paw prints bounded on the stairs. He wasn't alone and they were coming. I swallowed the rising bile in my throat and dashed to the window and scanned the lawn below to see a dozen werewolves stalking along the clearing perimeter. My arteries felt like mortar as I saw the creatures for the first time.

Wolves on steroids. That was the prevailing thought as I fixed my stare on them. They were about three times the size of a normal wolf with accentuated features – eyes like the arctic gleamed from bristling black skulls while sharp canines extended over fleshy gums. Their ears were tipped with silver and pointed slightly back, and their snouts cringed. I couldn't help but be slightly captivated as I watched them move purposely and with stealth. The way their massive joints appeared disembodied beneath thick fur was enthralling.

And unsettling.

I shuddered and my pulse raced as I unlatched the window and pushed it open. I turned to Leandra. She looked like death. "Go!"

Her eyes widened. "Are you mad? They'll eat us alive if we go out there!"

A series of loud growls tore through the house. My heart was an explosion as a deafening crash followed. They were breaking through the closed bedroom doors along the hall of the upper floor. I gave Leandra a shove.

"They'll eat us alive if we stay here."

She shrieked. A lusty howl rang out from below and she went to climb over the windowsill. She clung to the timber frame and froze as the door to our room splintered apart with a sonorous bang. The hairs on my arms spiked with the sound of a deadly snarl.

"J ... Jett."

I barely heard her as I whirled around to face a pair of tapering eyes. Hackles rose from the wolf's forehead, it snarled, exposing large ivory fangs. I could hear his pack moving through the cabin somewhere behind him. My breath slowed with the passing moments as I caught my reflection in the gold of his eyes.

Exhale.

He was a glorious looking beast, but he was no puppy. He growled and crouched low before his legs uncoiled in one rapid movement toward me. Saliva dribbled from his fangs as he sprang. Speed was my friend as I vaulted over him to land on top of the bed. Leandra made a loud noise as he charged at her. She leapt from the windowsill and onto the slanting roof as he slammed into the window opening. His jaws snapped on air. The timber window frame began to crack beneath his force. Howls like sirens cut through the night and Leandra screeched. Thunderous thumps shook the house as the werewolves outside began scouring the walls of the cabin to get to her.

"Jett!"

The cabin echoed to the thuds of canine feet. *Cavernous.* The others were coming, but there was no time to think. Seconds felt like forever. I let out a hiss and extended my talons. I sprung from the bed to ensnare the werewolf's neck. The impact was rough. My jaw slammed against wolf skull and I immediately went for his face, sinking my nails into his eyes.

I knew it to be their weakness. His big head writhed. My hands loosened and he managed to catch one between his jaws. The crunch was agony. I roared as my bones fractured and my skin ripped beneath the force of his jaws. I roared and plummeted a fist between his eyes. The blow gave me enough time to yank my other arm free. I clung on hard and shredded his ears with my fangs while hooking my talons deep into his nostrils. *Vice.* I had him caught. A blanket of red filled my vision. Violence surged. He was a solid mass of muscle. I gritted my teeth and sunk my talons deeper as the beast began moving backward.

My blood boiled with the coppery taste of wolf blood. His wiry hair stuck in my gums. A throaty snarl reverberated as he began to rise up on his hind legs. His body thrashed violently and the next thing I knew, I was winded and catapulting across the room at an alarming speed.

Boom.

I hit the wall hard and slid to the floor as he turned to regard me. *Breathe.* I gasped for air as he stretched to his full height of about eight feet. Black fur glistened as he arched his neck to growl so loud it hurt my ears. My heart stammered. I stood up as three more wolves burst into the room, and my legs almost buckled.

Dog meat.

We were goners. Leandra screamed. My ears buzzed as she scrambled back into the room. Twisting werewolf's jaws filled the window frame behind her. She dashed toward me and clung to my arm. I didn't notice her talons cutting into my skin as I looked at the alpha wolf who hovered dangerously close.

Shane.

It had to be him. More wolves spilled into the room like slinking shadows. Their eyes were a menacing glow over slobbering fangs as they surrounded us and waited for his cue. They appeared unearthly and sinister, yet they carried a certain magnificence. However, that was the last thing on my mind as Leandra trembled next to me. The alpha rolled his head and growled before he dropped to all fours and skulked closer.

Is this how it ends for us? Butchered by a primitive breed of Lygarou?

I think I'd rather starve in a filthy cell mocked by our food.

The air in the room was full of tension. I held the alpha's cold stare. It was Avila and Sun who filled my head as he snarled. His hot breath was rancid in my face. Leandra yelped as he growled roughly before lowering his head and adopting a strike pose.

I glanced at her. "Don't stop fighting until you have to."

Her eyes were wild when she nodded a reply. Her dark hair whirled as she faced the wolves and crouched lower, thrashing her talons through the air with a monstrous hiss. I mimicked her moves as the alpha went to leap at us. The other wolves took his cue and began to advance. I surged forward and braced myself for impact.

Silence. The room spun and my head tingled. I was still alive, and the wolves had vanished. *What the hell?* I frowned. There was a strange whimpering at my feet. My eyes darted to see a group of men and women writhing naked on the floor. Leandra's voice was a distant noise in my ear.

"W ... what just happened?"

I gaped and respite rippled.

"Clio, she came through after all."

Exhale.

19

VAMPIRES & WOLVES

Shane wore a pair of dirty jeans and nothing else. Tawny locks framed heavy-lidded eyes and weathered skin. His chest was broad, tattooed and flexed beneath a thick spread of matted hair as he approached me. The scent of wolf still lingered fresh on his skin.

"What the hell happened?" His dark eyes bulged. "What did you do to us and where the fuck is my family, blood-sap?"

We stood in the cabin living room. Leandra stayed close. The lighting was dim, but I saw them clearly. A handful of disgruntled Lystalkers stared with a dozen more outside with their wolf cousins. I was keen to get out of here and back to Avila. There was no way for me to know if she was still alive.

I gestured toward Blade and Athan whose remains still lay where they had perished. "I was sent here to kill your family. I killed them instead."

Ragged nails fingered a long goatee over a squared jaw. He barely looked at them. He took a step closer, fists clenched. Three of his men came up behind him. They each clutched a stake and all of them were shirtless, and they stunk like day-old urine. I tried not to grimace as he spat words in my face.

"What have you done with my daughter?"

"I've done nothing with her."

Frustration brewed like a red stain. He waved a fist.

"I'm gonna rearrange your smug vampire features if you don't tell me what I want to know." He flicked a wrist above him and one of his crew pushed a stake into his hand. He pointed the stake at my heart. "Where is she?"

"She is safe with her mother in Sweetwater Valley." I pushed the stake aside. "You don't want to go there, my friend. Trust me."

He had a nose like a Roman; strong and prominent.

"I don't trust vampires, or humans for that matter. You found a way to cloak her, didn't you? You found a way to stop the Lystalker change."

"Not me. A friendly neighborhood witch helped out.

It was either that or risk you and your kind eradicating humans altogether."

"Human survival is the least of my concerns after what they did to me." His voice was acidic. "Keeping me locked up for decades and using my blood to cause abomination. They're just all evil at heart … There's no hope left for humanity now."

"You're wrong, and your daughter is the key to undoing the damage caused by the use of your blood." I paused and my eyes bored into his. "Just not now."

"Why would you even care, vampire? You lost your heart the moment you turned kindred."

I nodded. "Maybe I did. Maybe I am the first of my kind to remember his heart and realize the power that lies in that space." I balled my fist and thumped my chest lightly. "Maybe, this is what the apocalypse was all about – something good must give rise from the ashes … from the bloodshed and violence. Something worth fighting for."

He gnawed at his bottom lip. His voice was gruff. "It's a loveless world."

"Not if we can find a way back to it."

His eyes flickered before he glanced at the men behind him.

"We will no longer turn on the full moon – you made sure of that. My pack isn't safe. When the vampire masters discover what you've done, they will hunt us relentlessly."

"If you remain elusive, they'll never know. Take your pack and go to Sweetwater Valley to be with your family. Bide your time and wait for the generations to produce the Blood Legend, then you will have your turn to take back the city with *heart* behind you." I smiled. "Surely the evolved Lygarou can co-exist with humans and vampires in the future?"

He laughed.

"You might well be the last of the dreamers." He paused and his eyes narrowed. "If we go, what will you do? My sources tell me that the clan have already begun constructing a dome over one half of the city. They will use humans as blood cows and slaves in their new world. Will you join them?"

"My place is with my daughter and the Mysticus clan. The plans for the future may not appear humane, but it will keep the Leavings generations alive long enough to see the Blood Legend come into fruition. Until then, I will remain as one of them."

"And after?"

It was my turn to laugh. "When the time comes, I will search for my woman in the afterlife. I won't stop until I find your daughter's grandmother again."

His jaw dropped as realization dawned. "Now I

understand."

"Yes. It was written in the stars with Scarla."

Leandra gave an exaggerated sigh. Her glossy lips pouted. "I have no idea what you guys are going on about, but I think it's best we leave while the night permits us to travel."

Ah, yes. Ignorance is bliss.

I grinned and silently thanked Clio. Leandra's memory of this fiasco was already fading with the cloaking spell. It was utterly superb.

She clasped her hips and tossed her hair. "What are you smirking about?"

I shook my head. "You're right, we must leave now."

I exchanged one last look with Shane. We had reached an understanding and there were no more words left to say. I gave a fast nod before making for the cabin door with Leandra. We paused at the top of the veranda stairs to see a pack of wolves patrolling the cabin clearing accompanied by about a dozen men and women in various forms of undress.

"What about them?" Leandra said.

The wolves gathered at the foot of stairs and peered at us. Pale blue eyes and crimping snouts. A series of high-pitched screeches broke the silence as bats soared across the night sky and the full moon hung like a cryptic illusion.

I fingered the vial of Shana's blood safely tucked away in my jacket pocket before reaching for Leandra's hand.

"Can you run with the bats?"

She nodded.

"Shall we?"

"Yes."

I wound my fingers around hers. We descended the stairs and the wolves parted to allow us through, and we became part of the night.

Dreamers were now for all the tomorrows. Whatever awaited us back in the city, I would always carry my stargazer, *my woman*, in my heart. It was her love that would be my strength and my salvation.

Jett's story is set to continue in *Blood Legends: Ascension* (Ground Zero: Book 3) and will be available to grab soon!

Blood Legends: Rebirth is a part of Kim Petersen's Blood Legends series. If you loved this story and want to be alerted when the next Blood Legends book is released, follow the link to subscribe to get exclusive Blood Legends email-alerts straight to your: https://forms.aweber.com/form/07/251088407.htm

Reviews are awesome and other readers when deciding on which book to read next! Please consider leaving a review of *Rebirth*: My Book

Kim Petersen is a USA Today Bestselling Author, author of The Ascended Angels Chronicles, and co-author of the Stone the Crows series. Her debut novel, Millie's Angel received a gold award in the 2017 Dan Poynter's Global eBook Awards.

Join Kim's Reader Tribe and Grab a Free Read: https://forms.aweber.com/form/72/1801730872.htm

Find Kim at:

Whispering Ink: https://whisperinginkpress.com/

facebook.com/kimpetersen11

twitter.com/kimpetersen_